I hoped no one could see her.

We were only two floors up. I stood behind her, slid my arms around her waist, and held her body close to mine. I was about to suggest that we go to bed, but I could tell by the look of excited anticipation on her face, she was looking forward to watching this fight.

I was so surprised. I would have thought she would have been the last girl to enjoy watching a good scrap. She was *too*... peaches and cream, too sweet, too nice, too proper, too damn middle class, and yet the anticipated excitement on her face made her look immensely sexy.

The fight erupted and Melanie let out a delighted cry. Her eyes were fixed fully on the two fighters; a curious smile spread across her face, and her breath came in short pants.

The fight was in full flow, punches swinging wildly. The crowd was obviously enjoying it and more groups of people rushed over to watch, including a number of girls who were clearly relishing the sight. Violence was in the air, creating a sexual excitement.

I should know, because I was being turned on by it. Not by the fight itself, but by the effect it had on the girls in the street, who squirmed with delight in their sexy and skimpy dresses and urged on the fighters; and also by my naked Melanie, whom I held in my arms and was being sexually energised by this display of male physical violence. My dark fantasy was becoming reality.

Also recommended...

You may also enjoy these other ForbiddenFiction works:

Spidermilk by Konrad Hartmann

Eddie Stover, private eye, lives in a future where artificial humans called LifeMates serve consumers as a purchasable commodity. When Stover takes a wandering daughter case, the search for the missing woman plunges him into a world of hijacked Life-Mates, psychedelic milk, and a bizarre spider-worshiping cult. As the thrall of his old addictions and the enticements of the woman he promised to protect threaten to consume him, Stover is faced with the realization that he cannot escape the choice love forces him to make. (M/F, F/F)

http://forbiddenfiction.com/story/kh1-1-000086

Deep Focus by M. L. Caufax

The university is prestigious, selective, and remote; high on a hill in the middle of a forest, it shelters its students from the distractions of the outside world. Yet, within its walls, a man with bright blue eyes and amazing powers of persuasion is conducting a private puppet show—using real people for puppets. Zöe's first year at college takes a surprising turn when she receives an ancient talisman for a Christmas present. When she discovers the shocking truth that she has been a mind-controlled sex slave, she fights back against the blue-eyed man with the help of the talisman and a fellow student, Trevor—the boy she once called Master. (M/F+)

http://forbiddenfiction.com/story/kh1-1-000086

Fighting Hard

B.B. Anderson

ForbiddenFiction
www.forbiddenfiction.com

an imprint of

Fantastic Fiction Publishing
www.fantasticfictionpublishing.com

FIGHTING HARD
A Forbidden Fiction book

Fantastic Fiction Publishing
Hayward, California

© B.B. Anderson, 2012

CREDITS
Editor: Rylan Hunter
Cover Design: Siolnatine
Cover photo: Carlodapino and Sergey Sukhorukov at Dreamstime
Production Editor: Erika L Firanc
Proofreading: Todd Michaels

SKU: BBA-000006-02 FFP
ISBN: 978-1-62234-278-5

Published in the United States of America

DISCLAIMER

This book is a work of fiction which contains explicit erotic content; it is intended for mature readers. Do not read this if it's not legal for you.

All the characters, locations and events herein are fictional. While elements of existing locations or historical characters or events may be used fictitiously, any resemblance to actual people, places or events is coincidental.

This story is not intended to be used as an instruction manual. It may contain descriptions of erotic acts that are immoral, illegal, or unsafe. Do not take the events in this story as proof of the plausibility or safety of any particular practice.

When I got into the courtyard, I found Estella waiting... there was a bright flush upon her face, as though something had happened to delight her.

Charles Dickens — *Great Expectations*

Contents

Chapter 1

Meeting the Catalyst

I first met Melanie at a party. As soon as my eyes fell on her, I was smitten. She was small and petite and with auburn hair down to her shoulders. She had a tiny nose, a perfectly formed mouth, and dazzling jade green eyes. She was as perfect as a porcelain doll.

As luck would have it, Melanie and I would turn out to have at least two things in common: a profession in journalism and a taste for voyeurism. Our profession in journalism was pretty standard stuff. It was our voyeurism which was a little out of the ordinary. It was a symbiotic and not very common type of voyeurism. Melanie would also cause me to have, finally, at *long* last, after a lifetime of sexual frustration, and at the age of thirty, ejaculation while having sex. These two factors—our shared voyeurism and how it led to me overcoming my impotency—are entwined.

She was the catalyst.

The party was being thrown by Keiko and she introduced us. Holding a glass of wine, Melanie smiled at me the sweetest of smiles and said hello.

"Pleased to meet you," I said.

"Likewise," she replied.

"Freddie is an editor," said Keiko. "Be nice to him as he buys some of my photos from time to time."

"And very good they are, too," I added, with sincerity.

"Thank you Freddie, you are a darling. Melanie is a journalist. Maybe you can charm this man into buying some of your writing. He loves being flattered. Massage his ego and he may commission a piece from you."

Keiko left us alone together.

"Is that true?" Melanie enquired. "You like having your ego massaged?"

"I am a man, so...." I shrugged my shoulders.

"Which magazine do you edit?"

"*London View*," I replied.

"Oh, the listings magazine. I've read it. It's very good."

"Thank you. I have a very good team. Keiko says you are a journalist. What sort of journalism are you involved in?"

"I'm on the staff of *Debbie*, the girls' magazine. I doubt that you are familiar with it."

"I know *of* it," I said. I did, too. I had seen it on the shelves in the newsagents. It was a magazine for girls in their early teens. "So how long have you been writing for *Debbie*?" I asked.

"Since I left uni. "

"Which is how long?" Taking a wild guess, she didn't look over twenty-two.

"Two years. I came to work for RG Publishers as a copywriter. After submitting countless articles for any number of their magazines, I got one published. I was so excited. It was about how to chat up a boy at a party, in case you are interested."

"Are you putting your advice into practice now?"

"No. If I was, I wouldn't be talking about myself. Actually, I should be following Keiko's advice and pitching myself at you, hoping you might commission me to write a piece." I laughed. I liked that answer. It was funny. "If you want to extend your market into young teenage girls, I'm your woman."

"Not quite our demographics, I'm afraid. However, if there are any uptight, middle class, politically correct, teenage girls that are not being catered for, we may be *just* the magazine to tap into that market."

It was her turn to laugh. "You don't think much of your readership," she said.

"You should hear my views on the staff."

"Maybe I should ask for their views on you?"

Keiko wandered over. "Is he being rude about his staff again?" she said. "Don't listen to him. He is a frightful boor. He wants to be editor of some awful right wing tabloid."

"There is nothing wrong with ambition," I said. "*London View* is a mere stepping stone."

As the party began to liven up, the chatter surrounding us became more animated and the laughter more spontaneous and frequent. Melanie and I sat at the end of a sofa. We chatted to our hearts' content, and Keiko, ever the perfect host, drifted in and out and of our conversation to ensure our glasses were full. Melanie and I had clicked instantly.

Later in the evening, Drum'n' Bass, a favourite of Keiko's, began pumping out of the music centre. It drowned out the general chatter and as talk became increasingly impractical, people began to dance. Defying convention, we didn't join in the frantic dancing and continued to chatter, despite the volume of the music. As we leant in close to one another, shouting into one another's ear to make ourselves heard, our bodies constantly made contact. Several times throughout the evening, a thigh was touched or an arm was brushed. Intimacy was engendered. At about three o'clock, —*where does the time go?*— the music went silent and the party quickly began to wind down. I decided to make a move.

"Look," I said, a little drunkenly. "If we are going in the same direction, why don't we share a taxi and I can drop you off?"

"It's very kind of you, but I think a taxi is a little extravagant just to get me home."

"I presume you live close by." She nodded and jerked her head in the direction I thought indicated Docklands. "You live in Docklands?" I asked. "In that case, may I walk you home?"

"No. I mean yes. What I mean is, *is, that* is my bedroom over there." She indicated a door behind me.

"You live with Keiko?" She nodded. "I had no idea."

"I moved in with her about six months ago. Her previous flat mate moved to Australia and so I moved in. I've known Keiko for some time. We have been friends for ages."

The party was over. The last of the guests were leaving.

I surveyed the room and said, "It looks like it's time for me to go."

She put her hand on my thigh, gave me a steady gaze, and said, "Do you have to go? You can stay here for the night." She leant forward, kissed me on the lips, and then pulled away. She leant forward again and this time I reciprocated. We kissed and her hand grazed my crotch, causing my cock to twitch and swell. She noticed it, smiled, and lightly

3

brushed it again. "Go on, stay."

After the last of the party had gone, Keiko came over and announced she was going to bed.

"I'll see you two lovers in the morning." She disappeared through a doorway, presumably into her bedroom.

Melanie took me by the hand and said, "Come on. I'm tired."

We rose and walked into her bedroom. She switched on the light. It was a neat room. There was a computer in the corner. Next to it was a table piled high with teenage magazines and with a red marker pen on top. A packed bookcase loomed over the double bed, which stood before me. My anxiety struck. The old fear bubbled to the surface from the depths of my subconscious.

Oh God! My little problem.

Would I be able to perform? Would my *problem* let me down, again? As always, I hoped against hope this time it would be different, that this time I wouldn't disgrace myself. A part of me wanted to make an excuse, to turn around and walk out. If I did, maybe, just maybe, I could save face. However, it was too late now. Anyway, I was determined to go through with this. I *wanted* to go through with it. I *wanted* to make love to Melanie.

Hell! I'm a man. I wanted to get laid.

Maybe this time it would be all right.

Melanie stripped off to her underwear, a matching bra and panties, smiled at me, then took these off, too. I hurriedly undressed until I, too, was naked. She switched off the light. A streetlight outside gave the room a dull glow. Melanie pulled back the duvet and climbed under it. I did the same.

We embraced and kissed. I ran my hands over the contours of her firm but lithe body, down her back, and over the soft mounds of her bottom. Her breath was warm on my neck. I slid down and kissed her breasts, going from one nipple to the other, with relish. Her nipples stiffened between my lips and she gave a soft sigh of delight.

I was hard. *Rock hard.* Nothing would have given me greater pleasure to thrust my prick inside her and start vigorously pounding away. However, I didn't.

Instead, I slipped down under the duvet and brushed my nose against her pussy. She was clean shaven and very smooth. Had she shaved before the party, I wondered? Had she hoped she was going to get laid? I parted her labial lips with my fingers and eased in my tongue. Her legs opened wide, allowing me maximum access, and I thrust my tongue deep inside her. As I touched her sensitive and swollen clitoris, she writhed above me and let out a soft groan. My fingers prised her lips further apart and my tongue delved as far as it would reach. The tip of my tongue started to tease the most sensitive part of her pussy. Each time it did so, she whimpered softly, delightedly.

While my tongue explored the pleasures of her femininity, I slid my hands under her and with my fingers caressed the soft mounds of her buttocks. Beneath me, her body squirmed on the sheets and her soft whimpers increasingly became more impassioned, turning into cries of rapture.

Suddenly, she swung her legs around my neck and forced me harder into her cunt, her body jerking upwards, her pelvis forcing itself up into my face. With a cry of uncontrolled ecstasy, her body thrashing as if in a convulsion, she let out an ear piercing scream and came violently.

Her body jerked violently, and then she slumped back onto the bed, exhausted, satisfied, and satiated.

The duvet had slipped to the floor. I pulled it up and covered us both with it. I lay beside her. She was breathing hard and I could see that her brow was covered with a thin layer of sweat.

"Did you enjoy that?" I asked.

"The best licking out that I have ever had. Some great tongue work there, I have to say." She turned onto her side, took hold of my prick, which was still rock hard, and said, "What about you? Have you some… unfinished business?" She gently stroked it, making it twitch.

I softly caressed her bottom, kissed her on the cheek, and replied, "Yes. In the morning. I want to sleep now, by your side."

She kissed me on the lips and we fell asleep in one another's arms.

I was the first one to wake up. Daylight made a feeble effort to shine through the curtains. I hurriedly swung my legs out of bed, stood up, and silently slipped into my clothes. My erection had long since died. I didn't even have a Morning Glory. As I did up my shirt, I looked at Melanie lying there asleep. She was so pretty in a cute and sexy sort of way. I crept out to the kitchen, which was cluttered with last night's party debris, poured a glass of water, and drank it. Leaning against the stainless steel sink, I gazed out of the window across the London sky-line. Not so far away, the towers of Canary Wharf loomed over Dock-lands. The sun gleamed off the windows of one of the towers, making me screw up my eyes.

"Morning," said a Japanese accented voice behind me.

"Morning Keiko" I replied, turning around. Keiko looked lovely. Ever since I had first set eyes on Keiko, I had always thought of her as a very pretty girl —*God! Two such lovely girls sharing the same flat. Somewhere in all this, lies a pilot for a sitcom.*— She had long jet black hair, sharply delineated cheeks, and a round face with a tiny nose and mouth. And, of course, large and lovely Asian eyes. She wore a silk kimono styled dressing gown with Japanese writing on it. It looked incredibly sexy on her.

"Did you have a pleasant night?" she asked, with a glint in her eye. Keiko spoke perfect English. She could pronounce the letter "L" with-out replacing it with the letter "R," and so did not pronounce the word *pleasant* as *present*, or *hello* as *hurro*, which is not something all her Japa-nese compatriots could do. Yet an undeniable accent lingered.

"I did. Did you?"

"I was alone."

"You should have joined us. It is a big bed."

"We'll leave that for your second date, shall we?"

"What about the third date? What shall we do about that?"

"Well you could try fucking me," said a voice from the living room. Melanie walked in wearing an oversized thick cotton dressing gown. She came up to me and kissed me on the lips. "Would you like coffee?"

"I shouldn't ask," said Keiko. "But, er, didn't you two... do any-thing last night?"

"I ate, then I slept," I replied, causing Melanie to burst out in a fit of giggles.

"Okay," said Keiko. "I'm not even going to attempt to ask."

We spent the rest of Sunday morning sitting around the dining room table chin-wagging. The two of them were quite chatty and perky and the time slipped by.

"Why don't you both get dressed," I said, "And I'll take you out to dinner," which I did. We bundled into a taxi and then went to a Japa-nese restaurant in Berwick Street, Soho. For the first time in my life I had

Sushi. I intended it to be my last as I found it inedible. Cabbages and raw fish mixed with rice, indeed! I couldn't finish it. Keiko even called me a fussy eater. Melanie and Keiko noisily lapped it up, though.

After the meal, we had a few drinks and then caught a taxi home. As I dropped them both off, Melanie turned round to me and handed me a scrap of paper. It had a telephone number on it.

"Call me," she said, smiling, and then the taxi pulled away.

Chapter 2

Analysis of My Problem

The second time I saw Melanie was the following Friday. After an editorial meeting, I texted Melanie asking her if she would like to go out with me. When she replied she would, I could have danced with joy! I thought she may have been a little disappointed the last time I saw her; I only gave her cunnilingus and not the, *ahem*, full service. Maybe she only wanted to go out with me so that I could finish off what I had started? Whatever the reason, I thought Melanie beautiful and charming and I had been thinking about her all week. I was keen to see her again.

I booked tickets for the play, *The Good Soldier Svejk* by Bertold Brecht, based on the novel by Jaroslav Hasek. During our lengthy conversation at the end of the sofa during the party, I discovered she liked the theatre and Brecht in particular. That the National Theatre was putting on a production of one of his plays was just the most perfect timing. Sometimes, some things just keep happening right.

That evening we met at the bar of the National Theatre. She looked stunning in a short white skirt that showed off the shapeliness of her thighs and calves. Red high-heeled shoes emphasised her pert little bottom. A red blouse hugged her form tightly. Whatever the quality of the play, I was going to have the most perfect company.

To my surprise, I found the play engaging. Afterwards, Melanie talked endlessly about Brecht and Hasek throughout the Thai meal we had in Soho. I knew about Brecht, but was unfamiliar with Hasek.

"I know about Bertie Brecht," I said. "He was a communist who travelled all the way across the Soviet Union just to get to America. Can you believe that? He travelled all the way through his utopian landscape in order to get to a country whose values he despised. Well, I suppose, at heart, everyone is a whore. I work for a magazine just to get the zlotys. What about Hasek? Was he another commie?"

"Hasek was an anarchist and was Czech, I think. He was an editor of a natural history magazine. He wrote articles about fictitious animals which he invented and because of that, he got the sack."

"A natural history magazine!" I said, bursting out laughing. "Poor sod! If I found myself an editor of a natural history magazine, I'd probably write articles about fictitious animals, as well, just to relieve the boredom."

After the meal, we ended back at my place. Compared to the tidiness of Melanie and Keiko's flat, mine was a tip. Books lay scattered over table tops. CD cases littered the floor. Newspapers and magazines lay piled against one of the walls. Even my print of George Grosz's 1934 New York Harbour had slipped and was at an angle. It was a wonder that the New York Harbour wasn't spilling out on to the floor.

However, I turned off the main lights and switched on a table lamp that both diminished the untidiness of the room and created its own atmosphere. I put on a CD of Lester Young being backed by the Oscar Peterson Trio, which created a nice and mellow ambience. I poured out a glass of white wine for each of us and we sat on the sofa, chatting about this and that, but mainly about Lester Young, whose music Melanie found intriguing.

Halfway through the second bottle, Melanie announced she was beginning to get drunk, put her hand on my thigh, kissed me gently on the lips, and said, "Why don't we fuck?" Again, her hand gently brushed my crotch. This seems to be a habit with her, and not a disagreeable one.

Well, what do I say to that? *Maybe another night, eh, love? I have a bit of a problem that may put a bit of a damper on the night's proceedings.* No! I kept my mouth shut and we went into the bedroom, undressed, switched off the light, and as before, climbed beneath the duvet.

We held each other and kissed and caressed each other's body. I slowly slid down her, kissing her neck, her breasts, and again, as last time, found my self giving her cunnilingus. She twisted her body away from me.

"No," she said.

I looked up. "What do you mean, no?"

"I want to be fucked properly. Stand up, by the bed."

I got up and stood by the bed, as instructed. My swollen prick was fully erect and stood out in front of me at an angle, like a flagpole protruding from a building.

She swung her legs out of bed and sat up so my prick was right in front of her face. Her legs were on both sides of me. She grabbed hold of my buttocks and pulled my prick into her mouth, and teased it with her tongue, her head going back and forth. She did this for several minutes, occasionally pulling her head back and examining my prick.

When she seemed satisfied, she lay down on the bed, looked me in the eye, parted her legs wide open, and said, "I want that huge cock in my cunt *now*."

I got onto the bed, knelt down between her legs, took hold of my prick, eased it in and started thrusting, back and forth, back and forth. Melanie screwed her face in ecstasy, urging me to fuck her harder and harder.

"Fuck me!" she cried out. "Fuck me! Harder! Harder!"

And I tried to do just that. Honestly, I did try my very best.

Sometimes best isn't good enough.

I just couldn't cum.

My prick was fully swollen and eager for action, but nothing was coming out.

Nothing. Oh God! Like a slow puncture on a bicycle, it started going soft. Again, my little problem.

I awoke the following morning. Melanie was perched on her elbow.

"Hello," she said. Light was pouring in through the window. She had obviously been up and pulled back the curtains. I thought of last night and my heart sank. Shit! Again! Why does this always happen to me? "It's a lovely day," she said. "Shall we go for a walk in the park, or shall we cuddle up under the duvet?"

I just wanted to die.

"Let's cuddle," she said laughing, as she cuddled up to me under the warm comfort of the duvet.

We embraced as she put her head on my chest and closed her eyes.

Having her warm, soft, naked body pressed against my own caused my prick to twitch, which was already swollen with a morning erection. She giggled and took it in her hand and started masturbating me. She looked at it with a smile on her face.

"One of the larger ones," she said with obvious authority, and carried on pumping it. Anxiety swept over me and it started going limp.

"It's not you, it's me," I said, turning away. I knew my face had gone red and I didn't want her to see it. "It must have been the wine we were drinking last night."

"Never mind" she said, kindly. "Let's get up and go outside for a walk."

We showered and then went down in to the park, which is opposite my flat, for a brisk walk. It was cold outside and a frost covered the windows; but the air was dry, so the frost was not thick.

Wrapped up against the cold weather, we walked gloved hand in gloved hand through the park. As we breathed out, our breath danced before our faces. It was a clear blue sky and a dazzling sun illuminated every blade of grass and outlined every naked branch. We had the park almost to ourselves, except for a couple of runners jogging. Melanie broached the question head on.

"Have you seen a doctor about... you know, your problem?"

Ah, such delicacy. *My problem.* My inability to ejaculate while having sex. A frustrated previous girlfriend had suggested I go and see a doctor about *my problem.* So I did. I told the doctor—a woman doctor as it turned out—which may not have helped. She recommended I go to a specialist and made an appointment for me to see one at St Thomas' Hospital. I didn't realise there were specialists for this sort of thing. Are they called *sexologists*, I wondered? However, I turned up at St Thomas' Hospital on the appointed day. There were quite a few of us queuing up to see this *sexologist*. I wondered what their problems were. Did any of them share my *little problem*?

When my name was called out, I walked in to the office and there was another woman.

Oh God! Another woman!

I couldn't help thinking this would be a lot easier if the sexologist was a man. She indicated the seat in front of the desk and so I sat down.

11

"How can I help you?" she asked, so I told her my problem. I told her I have no problem getting an erection when naked with a girl, but it goes no further than that. I cannot ejaculate. I cannot cum. I am fine when masturbating. When I have a wank, I can cum copiously. My sticky computer screen and keyboard can verify that. But put a woman in bed with me, even one as beautiful as Melanie, and I cannot cum to save my life.

I cannot with Melanie, and I could not with Jakki, nor with Cathy, nor Naomi, nor Gail, nor Polly, nor Nikki, nor Tania, nor Louise, nor Caitlin, nor Silvana, nor with any of the many one nights stands whose names escape me. As I spurted this out, — *oh dear, what an unfortunate choice of words* — my specialist *sexologist*, who sat attentively behind a desk, asked me what I exactly wanted from this session.

I said I wanted a pill that would enable me to cum when having sex with a woman. Instead of a pill, she gave me advice.

"Sometimes a sexual relationship needs time to build up," she said. "Don't hope for too much from a first time encounter. Work on it. Try various techniques like petting and caressing. Let it build up. If you go at it too quickly, you are maybe building up expectations that satisfy neither of you." She handed me a list of books. "I really think you would benefit from reading some of them. It will help you explain your anxiety and, in time, how to overcome it."

I felt she was missing the point, but I didn't want to say anything. I thanked her for her time and left her office. I threw the list into a basket on the way out. She had told me fuck all. If a sexual relationship some-times needs time to build up, what about one-night stands? I assume they do happen. What about men who go with prostitutes? They don't have time to build up sexual relationships. However, I hadn't been en-tirely honest with her and had held back. I hadn't told her what I fan-tasised about when I masturbated, my one recurring fantasy… and my only one. I had held *that* back.

Of course, I did not reply to Melanie's question in quite this detail.

I said, "Yeah, I went to the doctor. She said I need to work on my sexual relationships."

"I'll go along with that," she said, laughing.

I laughed, too, but deep down I was fraught with anxiety. There was a dichotomy in my sexual life. I wanted to cum when I had sex with

Melanie, but could not. However, I could ejaculate freely and copiously when I masturbated alone with *my dark fantasy*. It was only when I had this fantasy that I could cum.

I did not realise it then, but the two—Melanie and my sexual fantasy—would very soon come together, although it would take me down a road perhaps I didn't really want to go. However, I would rush down that road eagerly enough, gathering pace with each step.

Chapter 3

The Sweet Sadist

The road which I had no inclination to go down – *or did I?* – began the following Friday. That particular week had been busy. I had been frantically putting the magazine together and had not found the time to speak to Melanie apart from sending a few text messages. On Friday afternoon I arranged to go out with her. As a surprise, I got some tickets for a play, Noel Coward's Blithe Spirit, which I hated but she loved. Afterwards, she said, "Do you want to come back to my place? I can cook up a meal."

"I can buy the wine."

"I already have wine. Come on. Let's go."

I hailed a taxi and we went to her flat. Once there, I sat in the living room while Melanie busied herself in the kitchen. Keiko was out that night and I gazed around the flat as if it was my first time there.

It seemed much bigger and quite different without a party crowd heaving around. Pink curtains blended with a soft creamy white carpet. The flat had an undeniable aura of girliness. A huge print by Toulouse Lautrec hung above the fireplace: the one with the guy who has a giant red scarf wrapped around his neck. The picture was quite striking in the soft context of the rest of the room. There were some small Japanese prints, which were obviously Keiko's touch. Soft classical music played in the background.

Melanie had laid the table, lit candles, switched off the light, gave me a glass of wine, and told me to sit on the sofa. Every now and then, she would come in from the kitchen to check that I was all right, have a few words, and then hurry back.

"Do you like living here?" I asked on one of her brief forays to see if I was comfortable.

"The area's okay. The high street is just round the corner, so the shops are nice and convenient. We also have a night club in the street that can be quite noisy on Saturday."

"I can't hear anything."

"Oh, it's not the music that annoys me. It's that late at night, a lot of the revellers come rolling out and yell at the top of their voices, which is a bit of a nuisance." She then added cryptically, "Sometimes, though, it can be exciting."

I was just about to ask her what she meant by exciting when she dashed out to the kitchen again. It would not be long before I would find out exactly what Melanie found exciting.

For the first course, we had homemade pea soup, which was lovely. The next course was trout with almonds. Melanie was a fine cook. We finished with a homemade chocolate mousse, which again, was delicious. I found the wine a bit sweet, not that I said anything. However, Melanie stated she liked sweet white wine with any meal, even with red meat.

We retired to the sofa and she snuggled up to me.

Okay, this is it, I thought. I am going to have sex with Melanie. I should be able to perform all right. I had not masturbated in four days. My balls were heavy.

A thought ran through my mind, and not for the first time, either. What does Melanie fantasise about when she masturbates? I would find that out, too, soon enough.

We kept on talking in between whispers, caressing each other all the while. I caressed her legs while she ran her hand over my thigh, at one point brushing my prick. Eventually, we kissed. Her tongue darted into my mouth and we parried. I could taste her saliva. Her body was pressed hard against mine. I could feel her breasts squeezed against my arm.

I wanted to touch them, to fondle them, to take them in my hands and play with them and then put her nipples into my mouth, one at a time, and savour their flavour. I was getting an erection. Melanie noticed because she looked down, smiled, and then gently brushed her hand over my stiffening prick. Oh, that little trademark of hers.

"I think you're ready," she said.

"I've been ready all night."

"Me, too. I assume you have condoms." I took out a packet from my pocket and showed her. Her face lit up. "Good. Let's go to the bedroom."

We rose from the sofa and Melanie led me to the bedroom. This was the second time I had been into her room, but I only now noticed it was furnished with a white creamy carpet, pink curtains, and a pink duvet. I was the only masculine thing in this flat.

We stood in front of the bed and embraced and kissed one another. We got undressed and embraced again. I felt my cock stiffen. I caressed her bottom and wallowed in the feel of her naked breasts pressed against my bare chest.

"I'm sure you'll be fine tonight," she said, reassuringly. "Come on. Shall we fuck?"

"It would be silly not to," I replied. She laughed at that.

However, I was worried sick. My old anxiety thrust itself into the forefront of my mind. It had been bubbling away in the background all evening, but now the deed had to be done. The moment had come. Would it happen again? Would I be able to perform? Or would my manhood let me down, embarrass me, and finally, de-man me?

Just then, a noise arose from outside. An altercation was taking place in the street below.

Melanie smiled at me and said, "Interesting. Let's have a look."

She switched off the light, drew back the curtains, and we peered down into the street. Two young men were rowing about God knows what, but it was getting heated, and I just knew at any moment it would erupt into a fight. A crowd, who came pouring out of the nightclub around the corner, sensed excitement, and started to gather around.

Melanie stood at the window, naked and with one arm across her breasts and her other hand over her pussy. I hoped no one could see her. We were only two floors up. I stood behind her, slid my arms around her waist, and held her body close to mine. I was about to suggest that we go to bed, but I could tell by the look of excited anticipation on her face, she was looking forward to watching this fight.

I was so surprised. I would have thought she would have been the last girl to enjoy watching a good scrap. She was *too*... peaches and cream, too sweet, too nice, too proper, too damn middle class, and yet the anticipated excitement on her face made her look immensely sexy.

The fight erupted and Melanie let out a delighted cry. Her eyes were fixed fully on the two fighters; a curious smile spread across her face, and her breath came in short pants.

The fight was in full flow, punches swinging wildly. The crowd was obviously enjoying it and more groups of people rushed over to watch, including a number of girls who were clearly relishing the sight. Violence was in the air, creating a sexual excitement.

I should know, because I was being turned on by it. Not by the fight itself, but by the effect it had on the girls in the street, who squirmed with delight in their sexy and skimpy dresses and urged on the fighters; and also by my naked Melanie, whom I held in my arms and was being sexually energised by this display of male physical violence. My dark fantasy was becoming reality.

My cock swelled up, brushing Melanie's soft round buttocks. Melanie briefly turned away from the fight to look at me and smiled, put her hand behind her and started stroking my cock, and then turned back to the fight. She said nothing, but her breathing betrayed her excitement, and she simultaneously stroked me and relished the brawl. I had never known her to be so sexual.

The fight grew increasingly fierce, and suddenly Melanie murmured, "Look, blood."

I looked down and one of the combatants had blood splattered all over his white T-shirt. Melanie squeezed my cock even harder and I let out a groan. I ran my fingers down her belly and into her cleanly shaven pussy.

"Not yet," she said. "I want to watch the finish of this fight."

"Are you enjoying it?" I asked.

"Of course, I am," she said. "It's such a shame Keiko isn't here. She would have loved it. Aren't these two gorgeous? This is the best fight I've seen out here. Anyway," she added, breathlessly, "look at all that blood."

My cock in her hand was rock hard. I was close to orgasm.

Suddenly, one of the fighters was felled by a series of hard punches around the head, each punch accentuated by Melanie shouting," Yes! Yes! Yes! Kill him! Mash up his face!"

The fight over, Melanie's breathing was still coming in excited pants and her body, naked in my arms, was trembling. I looked down at the loser and he looked pretty badly beat up.

"Christ, look at him," I said, half in horror.

"I know," she replied. "I don't think I've ever witnessed anyone get so mashed up before."

It was obvious she had been thoroughly aroused by the sight. My cock was fully-erect and ready to cum.

"Melanie," I said. "I have to take you now."

"Go on," she said, "take me from behind."

I did. She leant forward and put her hands on the windowsill. I leant down to my trousers which were lying on the floor, removed the packet of condoms from the pocket, hurriedly removed one from the packet, tore off the cover, and slid the sheath onto my erect cock. I threw the packet onto the floor. Holding on to her waist, I carefully inserted my erect prick into her pussy and started moving back and forth, my pace increasing with each thrust. With each thrust forward, she would slam her bottom back into my groin. We built up a steady rhythm, which intensified with each thrust. Her pussy began to moisten.

As my thrusts became increasingly frantic, my whole body seemed to tingle as it raced towards a climax. I suddenly realised this was it. For the first time in my life, I was about to reach orgasm inside a woman. As the thought ran through my mind, it hastily dissolved as I gave one final thrust into her pussy and I exploded in a gigantic orgasm. A wave of ecstasy swept over me.

She threw her head back and cried out, "Oh Yes! Yes! Yes!" Seconds later, Melanie's body shuddered as she, too, came.

I continued to thrust until I was satiated and had nothing left. Her body jerked in short spasms and then she almost collapsed in my arms. I held her up, my arms around her waist. Instead of looking at me, she continued to look down at the scene below.

The fun was over. The crowd was beginning to move away. The gaggle of girls that I had seen with their skimpy skirts was walking away, giggling amongst themselves. They had loved it and so had my Melanie.

My cock was beginning to go limp. I withdrew from Melanie's pussy, tore off the condom and threw it into a wastepaper bin.

She turned round to look at me.

"Shall we go to bed now," she said.

I nodded. Melanie pulled the curtains shut and then we climbed into bed. We pulled the duvet over us and snuggled up to one another. In the dark, I could hear her breathing. It was beginning to settle into a more regular rhythm. So, at last, I finally had sex with Melanie. More to the point, I had finally had sex. However, the sex was completely different from what I had expected. I had expected that we would just fuck, but no.

I thought of the girls standing around watching the fight. Their faces were aglow. They found it exciting. They found it, like my Melanie, an aphrodisiac. I imagined they were wet; Melanie was. I felt it. I imagined they were just in the mood to fuck right now. The excitement it created in Melanie was intense. It was not me that bought her to orgasm, but the sight of two men fighting one another. Her eyes had been fixed on the spectacle the whole time.

The two faces of Melanie: Melanie the sweet as cherry pie girl. Melanie the seductive sadist. I found the contrast between the two to be wonderfully exciting. When I ejaculated in such a gush, and it practically ripped my body in half, I was being turned on by Melanie's reaction, which I found highly erotically charged. My first orgasm with a woman had matched my masturbatory fantasies. What an odd night this had been.

Melanie took my cock and slowly rubbed it.

"You still awake?" she asked.

"Yes," I replied. My cock began to stiffen.

"You were terrific tonight," she said.

"You were wonderful, too."

"Can you do it again?"

"I think so."

"Did you like the fight?"

"I suppose so. Did you?"

"Weren't they wonderful? They were like gladiators in the Coliseum."

"If you had a time machine, would you like to go to the Coliseum?"

"Do you have one?"

"No."

Her hand on my cock was getting more frantic and my cock became engorged with blood. She kissed me on the lips.

"Oh, I know that sounds terrible. Of course I wouldn't like to go to see men fight and die. But to see them fight, and to fight so brutally, well...." She smiled and left the rest of the sentence hanging in the air.

My cock was thoroughly swollen. Melanie threw the duvet onto the floor, got off the bed and went over to get the packet of condoms I had thrown onto the floor. She removed a condom, tore off the packaging, knelt on the bed, and slowly slid it onto my erect cock. She then climbed onto the bed, straddled me, and lowered herself onto my erection, which slid into her moist vagina.

As my prick touched her G-spot, she groaned softly. Grabbing hold of my shoulders, she closed her eyes and started jerking her body up and down, increasing the pace of the rhythm with each motion. I lay back and watched her soft breasts bounce rhythmically in time with one another.

Although the street light outside was not strong, I could see her body swaying above me. In the half-light, her skin tone and body took on a strange spectral appearance. She looked like a different person.

I took a breast in each hand and fondled them with my fingers. The nipples stiffened to my touch. Her arms slid around my head and she pulled my face into one of her breasts. Relishing the warm milky flesh, I took her nipple in my mouth, and started gently to tease it with my tongue, while my hand caressed her soft young bottom.

Melanie's vaginal muscles tightened and gripped my penis. This was a new sensation for me. I never knew vaginal muscles could contract and relax quite like that. Such control. My penis throbbed uncontrollably. I closed my eyes, thrust my body up, bucking Melanie, making her lovely breasts bounce forcefully, and came. Her vaginal muscles seemed to grip my penis as I ejaculated and squeezed every last drop of spunk out of my body. Never had I felt such pleasure. As soon as this was done, she threw back her head, arched her body, and lost herself in a spectacular orgasm.

Again, she cried out. Yes! Yes! Yes! I couldn't help wondering, as her eyes were closed, that in her mind, she was going, *Yes! Yes! Yes! Kill him! Mash up his face!* Was she reliving that moment of physical violence in her mind?

When she had finished, she fell forwards onto the bed, and buried her face in the pillow beside my head. Her ragged panting was loud in my ear.

"God, that was good," she said, slowly regaining her breath. She rolled over onto her back and lay beside me. She pulled me over so that my head was on her breast. It was beautiful. The best pillow I ever had. I could tell by her breathing that she had fallen asleep almost instantaneously.

I suddenly knew what she fantasised about when she masturbated. I also knew what she meant when she said, "Sometimes, though, it can be exciting." She meant the fights that break out outside her window. When one did break out, I imagined she would call out to Keiko who would rush in and, together, would watch them eagerly. I wondered how often fights broke out outside her window, and when they did, did she switch out the light and start masturbating, or did both girls masturbate together?

I pulled the duvet from the floor and dragged it over ourselves. I fell asleep, dreaming about Melanie, her eyes intense as she wallowed in the spectacle before her, her blood lust sated, and a cry of excitement as a gladiator fell, blood pouring from his chest, the thronging crowd roaring their approval. I shortly awoke with an enormous erection. The slow rhythm of her breathing made her breasts, soft beneath my face, rise and fall in unison. I fell back into a deep sleep and another erotic and dark dream.

Chapter 4

My Dark Secret

The following morning, I awoke to the sound of sizzling in a pan, followed by the distinctive smell of bacon frying. I opened my eyes and found the bedroom flooded with light. The curtains had been pulled back and the morning sun was streaming in.

Melanie stuck her head around the door.

"Morning, sleepy head," she said. "You want breakfast?"

"Caviar and wine would be very nice."

"It probably would be, but I don't have any caviar, and to tell you the truth, and at the risk of exposing my ignorance, I don't really know what caviar is."

"Caviar is fish eggs and I want two, sunny side up."

"We have eggs, but they came out the arse of a hen. Now, get the fuck out of bed and join us at the table."

She disappeared out of the room and back to the kitchen. How domestic, I thought. It was like being married. Actually, the sound of the bacon sizzling reminded me of my mother cooking breakfast when I lived at home with my parents. I got dressed into my clothes I wore last night (*would Melanie let me shower later?*) and combed my hair.

"It's ready!" Melanie shouted from the living room. "Come and get it."

I ambled into the living room. On the dining table were three plates of fried eggs, bacon, mushrooms and tomatoes. Melanie came in from the kitchen with two steaming cups of coffee. She was dressed in her oversized thick dressing gown.

"Tuck in," she said, and then with a twinkle in her eye added, "after last night, we need to get our strength back up."

22

She went over to the music centre and put on a CD. A classical version of *Greensleeves* came out of the speakers.

"Vaughan Williams," she said. "After the excitement of last night, we need something mellow to chill us out."

I thought it was another reference to our love making, but then I remembered the fight and Melanie's reaction to it. Maybe it was a reference to both.

I smiled, sat down and tucked in. The breakfast was beautiful. Melanie was a good cook. Good looking and good at cooking, I mused to myself: I must marry her. *She also likes to watch men fight.*

"Morning, Freddie" said a voice with a Japanese accent.

I turned around. It was Keiko. She sat down opposite me. She was dressed in her rather fetching and appropriate kimono dressing gown she wore the last time I saw her. I wondered if she wore anything underneath. I thought Keiko probably would look good naked. As it turned out, I would eventually be proved right.

After eating breakfast, we slowly sipped our coffees and spoke about nothing in particular. The Toulouse Lautrec gazed down at me. Greensleeves finished and another tune started, one I didn't know, but it was both very calming and stirring at the same time—*Fantasia* on a Theme by... someone or other. Melanie did say, but I can't remember. The coffee tasted nice in my mouth. The conversation between the three of us was easy going and natural. I felt at peace with the world.

"Oh, guess what happened last night?" said Melanie.

"Well, judging by the guest at our table, I have a pretty good idea."

"No, not that. Oh that as well, but something else. There was another fight outside in the street last night."

"Really," said Keiko, her face beaming. "A good one?"

"A good one."

"A very good one?"

"A very good one, in fact it was an excellent fight. The best one I've seen outside here, I think. They were going at it like warriors. There was blood all over them."

"Oh, I wish I had seen it," said Keiko, clasping her hands in front of her delightedly.

They both laughed and then Keiko turned to me.

"Did you see it?" she asked. I nodded. "Was it good?" I nodded again.

This conversation was giving me another erection. Luckily, the table hid it. I was in love with both these women, – but Melanie more so, obviously – because they displayed the qualities I most love in a woman when I masturbate: The qualities of prettiness and sweetness, girlieness and femininity, and the contrast of how they get sexually charged when they watch a display of manly violence. First Melanie and now Keiko. This was too much.

Of course, this was the dark secret I could not tell my sexologist.

My dark secret. My masturbatory fantasy. My flight of erotic fancy I conjure up when wanking: that a pretty and innocent looking girl, like Melanie or Keiko, gets a sadistic sexual arousal when watching a fight. In my mind, I always conjure up the image exactly: the sweet and innocent face; the eyes wide with interest; the tongue licking the lower lip; and the mouth upturned slightly in a smile. As the fight heats up, as blood begins to flow, she becomes increasingly excited and sexually aroused. Her pussy moistens. Her body tingles with delight.

Then the kill.

As blow after blow rains down on the loser, as the winner pulverises the whimpering loser into a bloody pulp, she silently has an orgasm, and at that point, with my hand frantically tugging my swollen cock, I jerk myself to satisfaction. It has always been and always was this fantasy. No other. None at all. Just this.

And here I was, with two women who exactly fit my ideal fantasy. My erection forced itself against my trousers. I had done exactly what my sexologist had told me to do: worked on my sexual relationship. She would have been so proud.

The conversation, thankfully, moved on. I had become mute. To take part would have betrayed my excitement at theirs. Later, when my erection had died down, Melanie and I showered and dressed. We left Keiko at the flat when her boyfriend called in. I remembered him from the party. He was called Harvey and we spoke briefly. He was a boxer. I remembered her previous boyfriend. He was also a boxer.

We strolled hand in hand down the road. The road was lined with Victorian houses that had mostly been converted to flats. Melanie and Keiko's flat was a top floor conversion. We reached the end of the road. On the corner was the night club Melanie had told me about.

"I suppose our two fighting boys spilled out of this club," I said.

"I wonder how they are," she said. "One of them got really mashed up last night."

Mashed up! That was a favourite phrase of hers. I thought about her reaction to the fight. She had enjoyed it, *really* enjoyed it. It was something sexual. That was obvious. It wasn't just sadism or cruelty. Or were sadism and cruelty sexual? I must read up on my *Marquis de Sade*. When she came to orgasm, she had not been concentrating on me; her eyes had been fixed on the scene of violence taking place in the street below. It energised and excited her and this fed into her love making. It should have shocked me, but it didn't; it excited and stimulated me.

She found men fighting a turn-on and because of that, I found her a turn-on. Where is this going, I wondered?

Where indeed?

"Do you know any restaurants," I asked.

"Not really. Let's just stroll along and see if we can find a place."

We strolled past a McDonalds, a Safeways, and a Chinese restaurant—no, she didn't want Chinese. We eventually stumbled across a Portuguese restaurant.

"How about this?" she asked.

I said fine and we went in and sat at a table. I had never tried Portuguese food before and was curious to know what it was like. The restaurant was smart in a typical restaurant chain sort of way—neat rows of tables, padded benches to sit on, and red décor everywhere—but there was no sign of it being particularly Portuguese. The food, which Melanie chose, was a fish stew, and quite lovely.

Over the meal, we discussed the Coward play that we saw the previous night. It had only been last night, but it seemed to belong to the distant past as so much had happened. With the discovery of Melanie's other side—her love of manly violence—I had trouble focussing on what she was saying: Something about her admiration for the sets.

After demolishing a bottle of Portuguese wine, we went to a pub where everyone seemed to know Melanie. We sat down on an overstuffed leather sofa with our drinks. There was a newspaper and magazine rack. She picked up a copy of the *Times* and I picked up a copy of the *Mail on Sunday*. We read to ourselves for twenty minutes, reading out snippets that we thought the other might find interesting.

"Look at this," she said. I looked up from the paper. She handed me a copy of the *Times* magazine. I put the *Mail on Sunday* down on my lap and took the magazine. I thought it would be open on the theatre section, as I knew her love of the theatre. Instead, it was open at the sports section.

"Read the main article," she said.

The article was Cage Rage, or Ultimate Fighting.

"I want to go and see it," she said excitedly.

"It's on at the Royal Albert Hall."

I had never even been to a boxing match, let alone an Ultimate Fighting Competition event. On my mobile, I rang the Albert Hall and ordered the tickets. The event was not for another couple of months.

During those next couple of months, the ties between us remained strong. I was determined not to lose Melanie. So I was attentive towards her, but gave her plenty of space. I treated her, but not too generously, in case I should overdo it. In truth, my fondness, or crush, if you prefer, was driven by a sexual desire that consumed me like a fire; but I didn't let it show. I hid it behind a mask of unassuming attentive caring. I did not let on that she was the only woman I had ever met who could bring me to full sexual fulfilment, who could, in short, make me ejaculate during sex. I thought she might find that a bit weird.

Yes, our sex life carried on. No more embarrassing moments. No going soft at point of entry. No more drooping while on the job. When having sex, my mind would be alive to that night and that morning, when during the fight, her blood lust was up and she became the most sexually stimulating woman in the world. I would cum and cum.

As for the conversation between Melanie and Keiko the following morning, that created a picture in my mind I kept for myself when I had a quiet wank. I would picture them together, alone in the flat, naked, cheering on a savage fight in the street below, squirming with delight with each savage blow, relishing the blood smeared bodies, and then falling into bed together, still naked. Maybe Melanie was not the only woman who could bring me to full sexual fruition.

I thought of Keiko. Like Melanie, and like many girls from the Far East, she was sweet, pretty, and polite. Like Melanie, she had a blood lust that seemed to go against her nature, but because it did, and because of its intensity, made her sexually charged.

Keiko is a talented sports photographer and as Editor of *London View*, I commissioned her work many times, usually for the sports pages. That's how I met her. She managed to capture that special moment in her photographs. The ball being caught by the fielder; the net being stretched by the ball after having thundered past the shoulder of the goal-keeper; the look of despair on the tennis player's face after having fluked his serve and conceded the game to his opponent; and the anguish on the face of the golfer as his ball just misses the hole. It is these moments, that human touch, which has gained her such a reputation.

I might not be able to hold on to her for very long. Even though she has only been in this country for four years, she is beginning to capture the attention of the heavy media: her pictures have recently been running in *Scotland* on Sunday, *The Independent*, and the *Sun*. I remembered a series of photographs she had presented to me.

It was a feature on the up-and-coming heavyweight championship boxer, David "The Iron" Smith. He fought with James Lewis and after six gruelling rounds, managed to pulverise him into submission. I commissioned Keiko to take the photos and had been struck by the dramatic quality of all of them.

One in particular, and one which I used in the magazine, showed David "The Iron" Smith slamming his fist into the face of James Lewis. Lewis' face was contorted out of all shape by the blow. Blood and sweat flew into the air. The brutality of the fight had been perfectly captured.

When I discussed the photos with her, I noticed how she talked with relish about the fight, how she gave a delightful laugh as she recounted how blood had been splattered on her blouse as she took that photograph. It makes sense now. How she must have gone home and recounted that story to a delighted Melanie.

I realised how alike they both are. It was easy to see why they would make perfect flat mates. I was not to know, of course, but I was being particularly perceptive. How alike indeed. How much more so than I had imagined.

However, during the next two months, we were, for all intents and purposes, a normal couple, an item, with nothing perverse about us at all. Oh but perversity has a habit of bubbling away beneath the surface and when you find someone whose perversity matches yours; it can start gushing like a freshly dug oil well.

In those two months, we met every Friday and usually spent the weekends together, either at my place or Keiko's, who didn't mind me staying over. Indeed, Keiko always seemed pleased to see me. Melanie and I busied ourselves by going to the theatre or the cinema. We went to the opera once. Our sex life was just fantastic.

Two months later, we went to see Cage Rage at the Royal Albert Hall.

Chapter 5

A Proposition

On the night of the fight, we met up with Keiko at the bar in the Royal Albert Hall. Keiko had been hired by a rival London magazine to take some photographs. She sat at a table with a camera around her neck and a large bag beside her. She wore a green sleeveless jacket with lots of pockets which held accoutrements necessary for her camera. She looked as if she was going to take photographs of wild life in deepest Africa.

"Hello," says Keiko to both of us, and then looking at Melanie, added, "You look beautiful this evening."

She did, too. Melanie wore a red backless dress that came down to her ankles but was split up one side. It revealed a bare left leg, a naked back, and ample cleavage. Tasteful, but discreetly, sexy.

"Thank you," said Melanie. "I see you're here to work."

"Yeah. I was lucky to get this assignment. There is quite some crowd out there. I am sure that it is sold out."

Keiko was right about the crowd as there were quite a number of people mingling in the bar. As you would expect, there were a lot of men, but there was a substantial number of women, as well. Some, like Melanie, were with men; but there were also groups of girls on a girlie night out. After all, how much more girlie can it get than to spend an evening watching two semi-naked testosterone charged hunks beating the crap out of one another?

"I have to go. See you guys later," said Keiko, who lifted up her bag and made her way to the ringside.

Melanie and I went into the auditorium and took our seats. We were about halfway up in the stands; row Q, seats 25 and 26. From where we were, we could see Keiko at ringside, setting up her cameras.

"Excited?" I asked.

"Yes," she replied. "Are you?"

"Yes," I replied with all honesty; but it was not the prospect of the fights that excited me, but the proximity of Melanie and the anticipation of the hoped for reactions while she watched the fights. She linked up her arm with mine and snuggled up close. This was more like it.

"I haven't even been to a boxing match, let alone UFC, so I don't really know what they're like."

"You've never been?" she said.

I shook my head. "Have you?"

"Yes. Both Keiko and me."

"Keiko?"

"Yes. We usually come as members of the audience; but as you can see, she is working tonight. Anyway, I'd rather come with you," and she gave my arm a squeeze.

"What are these things like?"

"These *things* are wonderful. They have loud music which pumps you up full of excitement, then the fighters come on with a big fanfare, and then the fun starts."

"They fight."

"Yes. Sometimes the fights aren't so good. One fight I saw lasted less than eleven seconds. It was a knockout. By the way, the eleven seconds included the ten seconds it took to count him out. Well, where's the fun in that? Sometimes they just end up wrestling each other while on the ground. Again, really boring. But when they get into a real slug fest and the punches are coming thick and furious and their blood is up, then it can become deliciously violent. That is when it becomes good."

Deliciously violent.

I looked around me. All the seats were taken. The Royal Albert Hall was suddenly plunged into darkness. The Octagon in the middle of the hall became flooded with light. A cheesy power ballad from the eighties, I couldn't identify which one, was blasted out from the speakers and reverberated around the hall. A camera on a crane relayed what was happening in the ring onto large giant screens at the back of the hall.

A man wandered into the ring. He was big and burly with close cropped hair. His face betrayed an air of arrogance. He wore a dinner jacket and bow tie.

"Ladies an' gen'lemen," he said in a coarse cockney accent. "Welcome to the sixth Ultimate Figh'ing Championship competition." There was a huge roar of applause. Even Melanie started clapping enthusiastically. "Welcome to Cage Rage!" he bellowed. Another roar of applause exploded, threatening to drown out the music.

"Any wimps in the audience?" A moment's silence. The MC screwed up his ugly face contemptuously. "Good. 'Cause if there is, then they can fark orf!" Another roar of applause.

"Fark off! What a charmer, eh?" I shouted at Melanie. I had to shout at her because of the noise. She laughed, but I could see she was taken in by this vulgar showman.

He introduced the first fight. Separately and one after the other, two fighters trotted down a pathway from the changing room to the ring. Each had his own entourage that trotted behind. There was a huge fanfare and roars of approval from the audience who were well and truly hyped up. The preliminaries seemed to last forever. Each fighter was interviewed (why?) by the brute in the dinner jacket and each fighter bragged about his fighting abilities. The ring girls flounced around like fishes in a net. All of a sudden, the ring was cleared and the fight was on.

Beneath the glare of the lights above them, the fighters circled around one another. The camera on the crane focused in on them like a bird of prey. I glanced at Melanie. She, too, was focused intently on the two men, her eyes wide and her mouth slightly open. My cock slowly began to stir. The audience sank into an expectant quietude.

One of the fighters' lunged against the other and they wrestled, but no blows were exchanged that made contact. It was the first of three rounds. The first round came to an end. I was surprised. I thought it was just a free-for-all scrap. But no, there are rules.

The second round started and again they faced one another. Blows were exchanged. There was a brief contact with fists and an expectant cheer from the crowd which quickly died away when the expectant fist fury was not followed through. They ended up wrestling each other to the ground.

It was not until the third round when things began to liven up. One of the contestants lurched forward, hit the other one in the face and followed it up with a series of blows. The crowd burst into life and roared its approval.

Melanie's grip on my arm tightened and from the corner of my eye I could see her lean forward with an excited glint in her eye.

The one doing the punching got his adversary against the side of the cage and started raining down blow after blow.

Melanie jumped out of her seat and cheered him on.

The fighter taking the blows collapsed to the ground and slapped his hand on the canvas. *Submission.* The fight was over and everyone stood up and applauded.

Melanie sat down, hugged me, and then rested her head on my shoulder. I could feel her breathing coming in short, excited pants. I felt a twinge in my trousers. What greater arousal can there be than Melanie being excited by male violence.

Two more fights followed. They were pale, unsatisfactory affairs. The crowd was restless. Melanie, for whom, after all, I had bought the tickets, seemed slightly bored. A fourth fight proved more exciting and included a knockout, which was quite dramatic and seemed to please Melanie. By the end, she was snuggled up to me like a giant pussy cat, as if we were at the cinema watching a romantic comedy.

Even the main event didn't prove all that exciting. The fighters spent a lot of the time rolling around the ground like kids scrapping in a playground. There was even some booing from the crowd and shouts insisting the referee make them stand up and fight. I, too, had become bored. My cock had become limp with Melanie's evident lack of excitement.

Afterwards, I waited outside for both Melanie and Keiko to come back from the Ladies. I had told Keiko I would give her a lift back. When they came out, I noticed they were both stopped by a group of girls with whom they both seemed to be on familiar terms, which surprised me. They chatted and laughed for a couple of minutes and then came over and joined me. As we strode down the steps of the Royal Albert Hall, crowds mingled outside. Across the road, Prince Albert was in his imperial splendour beneath a stone canopy.

"Did you enjoy the fight?" Keiko asked. "I got some great pictures. I have to download and email them to the magazine tonight. So you two: not too much noise while I'm working, if you know what I mean."

I drove back to their flat. Melanie sat beside me and Keiko in the back.

As I drove beneath the yellow street lights through South Kensington, I said, "You know what, Melanie? You should write about sport."

"Sport? Are you kidding? What do I know about sport?"

She was right, but it was an idea that just came to me, half as a joke. But the more I spoke about it, the more I could see the idea begin to take hold in Melanie's head.

"Sure, you don't know anything about sport; but you're a journalist. You could do research. After all, Keiko takes pictures of sporting events, but what does she know about sport?!"

"I know a lot about K1," piped in Keiko.

"What's K1?" I asked in all innocence.

"What you have just spent the evening watching," replied Keiko, with a wry smile on her face.

"UFC is also known as K1," added Melanie helpfully. "K for knockout. 1 for number one sport. And Keiko knows an awful lot about it."

"That is as maybe, but she knows nothing about tennis, football, and loads of other sports, and yet she goes to these events and takes photos. Damned good ones, as well."

"Thank you," said Keiko, looking genuinely pleased with my comments.

"You, Melanie, as a journalist, can do research. You could research a piece about K1."

"*Mmmmm*," she murmured, and then added, "I will have to think about it."

We arrived at the flat. Keiko went into her study and I heard her switch on the computer and set everything up to download the pictures she had taken. Melanie went to the drinks cabinet and poured everyone a drink. As Keiko busied herself at the computer in her study, Melanie sat beside me on the sofa.

"I've been thinking about what you were saying," she said, "and you know what? I wouldn't mind having a go at writing a piece about K1."

"Well, go for it," I said encouragingly. "What have you got to lose? After all, it is a subject that interests you."

"Thank you for a splendid evening. I really did enjoy myself. I want to go to bed. Coming?"

"I'm right behind you."

We went into Melanie's bedroom, undressed, and then slid under the duvet. We didn't make love that night but just lay in each other's arms. Melanie fell asleep almost instantly. In the background, I heard the sound of Keiko downloading her photographs into the computer. The sound gently faded into nothingness as sleep overwhelmed me.

Chapter 6

A Revelation About Keiko

Three weeks later, over the dinner table in the girls' flat, Melanie handed me a manuscript. It was an article on Cage Fighting. I hadn't thought she would go through with it, but she had.

"When did you write this?" I asked.

"I wrote it in the evenings, on the weekends, and when I was at the office pretending to be working. You're an editor. Tell me what you think and whether it is publishable or not?"

So I read it. It was not a bad piece. I had seen some of her work in *Debbie* magazine so I knew she could write. Of course, you don't get a job as a staff writer on a magazine unless you know how to write, and write well.

"Melanie, this is very good. But it won't get published. For one thing, there are no interviews. Secondly, everything in here has been said before. There is nothing new."

"So I need a new angle?"

"Right. Something that hasn't been said before. Something that an editor can say: 'Hey, this is new. This is something I can pitch to my readers.'"

Shortly afterwards, she left the staff of *Debbie*, the girls' magazine, and joined the staff of *Raunch*, a ladette's magazine, which was quite a difference from her old job. Whereas before she was dealing with the problems of her readers' boyfriends, now she was dealing with her readers' problems of getting laid and how to survive a night of binge drinking without getting arrested. Typical articles are which movie star you think has the biggest cock and which R'n'B star would you like to fuck. That kind of thing. *Raunch* was a bit like *Loaded*, but for girls.

I imagined the editorial offices of *Raunch* to be full of the ladettes to whom they were pitching their magazine, but when I went to collect Melanie one day for a dinner date, I found an office full of girls like Melanie: young, intelligent, well spoken, well behaved, well-bred, and decidedly middle class. Although, admittedly, pump up those same girls with alcohol, and I may have seen something quite different, but I had my doubts.

Melanie took my advice to heart, and three months later, we were lying in bed when she handed me the latest edition of *Raunch*.

"I have a piece in it," she said proudly.

"You always have pieces in it. You're one of the staff writers."

"This is different. I have a main article in it. I have also written about someone you know."

Intrigued, I flicked open the magazine to the contents page, scanned it for Melanie's name, found it, and turned to page 42. The headline was *"I love having sex with UFC fighters says UFC groupie.... And I'm not the only one. There are lots of us. A special report by Melanie Matthews."* I settled down to read the article.

Yukiku Furajami is a Japanese photographer who came to London four years ago, This must be Keiko she is talking about. The name had been changed.

...but if photography is her livelihood then watching men punch each other in the face, gouge out their eyes, and then beat each other into submission is her passion and pastime.

The article went on about how Yukiku went to all the fights and then had sex with all the fighters.

This was Keiko all right. There was a photograph, which, despite having the girl's face pixated, was very obviously Keiko. One picture had her dressed in an incredibly skimpy dress — yes, I have seen it on her several times before — hugging a semi-naked brute of a man with bulging muscles, long curly hair, and a torso smeared with blood. His face had also been pixated. Although the man was obviously a model and made to look real, Keiko had used herself as a model. I glanced down at the copyright by the photo. It said: *Copyright Keiko Hanako.* As I thought: Keiko had taken the pictures herself.

As I sat naked in bed next to an equally naked Melanie, I carried on reading her article. It was more of the same, how she and her friends relished watching men fight and how they competed to have sex with the fighters afterwards. My penis began to swell uncontrollably.

I put the magazine down. My erection formed a tent where it propped up the duvet.

"What did you think of it?" Melanie asked hopefully.

"It was very well written. Well done."

"Thank you."

"Yukiku is Keiko, isn't she?"

"Yes. Is it that obvious?"

"Well, the photograph gives it away."

"It's pixated."

The copyright isn't." I turned off the light, slid under the covers, and turned over and faced Melanie, who was facing me. The street light outside made her face appear ghostly. "Is Yukiku, sorry, I mean Keiko, a K1 groupie?"

"Yes."

"So she likes…"

"Fucking fighters," she said, completing my sentence with a smile.

"I would never have guessed."

"Wouldn't you?" she said, and then, under the duvet, her hand held my prick, which was fully erect. "Her present boyfriend is a boxer and so was her previous one."

"It is a bit of a giveaway, I suppose."

"Now that you know what she's like, what do you think?"

"What do you mean?"

"Does the idea… excite you? I only ask because your prick is fully erect after reading my article and I don't suppose it's my writing style that is turning you on… and let's face it, it's obvious you are well and truly turned on." She gently massaged my erect prick as if to emphasise her point.

I said, "Does the idea… excite you?"

"What?" she said, grinning. "Does the idea of Keiko being turned on by men fighting excite me? Not really."

"No. The sight of men fighting. Does *that* excite you?"

She cuddled up to me, kissed me on the lips and caressed my bottom.

"Darling. You know it does. I'm not blind. I'm not stupid. I know

37

you used to have trouble ejaculating when you had sex with women. I fully realise that *your little problem* was not resolved until the fight outside the window that night we fucked... and I also realise it was not the fight that turned you on. Am I right?"

"Yes. You are completely right."

"I know what the trip to the UFC was all about and I knew at the time... but that's fine. I got turned on: you got turned on. We're both happy."

With the air cleared, she pushed me onto my back, mounted my erection, let my prick slide into her vagina, and started riding me, jerking her hips back and forth, and her soft pert breasts bobbing up and down. Then she got off me and flopped back down on the bed.

"Fuck me," she cried out. "Fuck me hard. Hard!"

We embraced each other passionately. Feeling the softness of her skin, the warmth of her flesh, my scrotum became taut as my prick swelled. It was twitching, eager for action.

Melanie wrapped her legs around me, gripping me tightly. I slid my prick into her cunt and I started thrusting. She let out desperate, heartfelt moans. I responded to her cries with increased thrusting.

"Harder!" she begged. "Harder! Fuck me harder!"

She ran her hands down my back as I fucked her, held my buttocks with both hands for long appreciative moments, before gripping my neck and holding me tightly to her, so my face was buried in her hair. I plunged in deeper, gripping her bottom with both hands so I could thrust more forcefully.

I could sense the lust swelling through her clit, her vulva, and her labia. Her rapid breathing betrayed the excitement pulsating through Melanie. Excitement gave way to ecstasy, galloping like wild horses until she came, letting out an ear-splitting scream that threatened to shatter the very window panes and to get Keiko rushing in to see if I was murdering Melanie. Her fingers dug into my back like claws, her pelvis jerked into me, forcing my arse into the air.

At that moment, I thought of Keiko at the UFC, relishing the bloody violence unravelling before her and then joining the fighters backstage afterwards and fucking them. I came, forcefully, ejaculating every last drop of spunk until I was spent.

We collapsed on the bed. I lay on top of Melanie's body, which was warm and soft. Her excited breathing was beginning to relax, and I felt a great weariness overcome me. I slid my arms around her waist and laid my head on her soft breasts.

"That was good," she said, running a hand through my hair. Her eyes were closed and I could tell by her breathing she was on the verge of sleep.

"I loved the article," I said.

"I know you did," she replied.

"Just one question."

"Go to sleep my darling. We're both tired."

"Just one question."

"What is it, darling?"

"Did you actually see Keiko backstage with the fighters?"

"Yes, I did."

"Does she sleep with them?"

She opened her eyes.

"Yes, she does. Does that excite you?"

"Would you like to sleep with them?"

"No," she murmured after a second's pause. "I have you to sleep with."

"If you didn't have me, would you like to sleep with them? Would you become a K1 groupie?"

"It depends. I don't know. Go to sleep, darling." She closed her eyes and was asleep.

I felt ashamed of myself that I had made love to Melanie while thinking of Keiko cheering on a fighter and then fucking him afterwards. I just found the idea of Keiko being a K1 groupie a complete turn-on.

But what of Melanie? Would she ever go to bed with a K1 fighter? Has she ever done so? Could she become, like Keiko, a K1 groupie? Has she, in fact, ever been one?

I didn't know the answers, but the questions intrigued and excited me. I fell into a deep sleep and dreamt of Melanie and Keiko pleasuring a K1 fighter in his changing room. I was beginning to find both girls equally exciting.

I woke up the following morning and found the bed empty. I put on my dressing gown that now hung permanently behind Melanie's bedroom door and wandered into the living room. Melanie and Keiko, also in their dressing gowns, were on the sofa cupping their morning coffee. They had been talking and both greeted me with mysterious smiles. I smiled back and went to the kitchen, poured myself a mug of coffee, strolled into the living room and sat down in the armchair. Melanie and Keiko were opposite me, as if I was having a job interview.

"Did you like Melanie's article?" Keiko asked.

"Very good," I said. "I don't know which name suits you better — Keiko or Yukiku?"

"It depends whether I am incognito or not. For our regular morning coffee, I am happy to accept the name Keiko."

"Freddie finds it exciting that you're a K1 groupie," said Melanie.

"Does he?" replied Keiko, giving Melanie a knowing look. "Am I the sort of girl you like then, Freddie?"

"I think you are," said Melanie. "I better watch out for you two. I'm no longer leaving either of you in the flat together and alone."

"Oh, I wouldn't worry," said Keiko. "I think he has found exactly what he wants."

I nodded. It was obvious Melanie had reported back to Keiko about the conversation in bed last night. I got the impression I was being teased about it; but since there is nothing wrong with being teased by two pretty girls, I enjoyed the moment.

Keiko was right, though. Melanie is the sort of girl I like, and all three of us — Melanie, Keiko, and I — knew this. But since Melanie is like Keiko, and Keiko is like Melanie, it meant I liked them both. I wondered if last night we'd actually cleared the air or had just complicated things even further.

Chapter 7

Meeting Eddie Fucking Monahan

I first met Eddie Monahan in The Gay Hussar, the only Hungarian restaurant, as far as I know, in London. Melainie and I sat in the corner of the restaurant waiting for our goulash to arrive when a hulking great bulk of a man mountain wandered in. Melanie looked up.

"Good lord!" she exclaimed in surprise. "It's Eddie. Eddie Monahan."

The man mountain, hearing his name, turned our way, and with narrowed eyes, gazed in our direction. When he saw Melanie, he gave a huge smile and came over.

"Melanie. How are you?" His voice seemed to surge from the depths of the earth.

"Fine, Eddie. And you?"

"Not so bad."

"Let me introduce you to Freddie. Freddie, this is Edward. Edward, Freddie." He looked at me with narrow eyes, as if trying to measure me up, and then extended his hand across the table. We shook hands. "Why don't you sit down and join us?" suggested Melanie. I wasn't bubbling over with enthusiasm at that suggestion, I can tell you. Don't ask me why, but he gave me the impression of someone who could be your best friend one moment and your worst enemy the next. An air of violence hung around him like a malevolent cloak.

"That's very kind," he said, "but I can only stay for a couple of minutes. I'm expecting my friend any moment now."

"Darling," Melanie said, turning to me. "You might remember Eddie. He fought at the UFC at the Royal Albert Hall when we went there early this year. He won his bout, as you may remember."

I could neither remember him nor any of the other fighters. Through every bout, my attention had been focussed on Melanie. However, I didn't want to piss him off so I made out that I recalled him vividly.

"Oh, yes, of course I remember. Very good fight. Congratulations."

He smiled back appreciatively.

"Are you in the fight game?"

"No, no. I'm in journalism."

He turned to Melanie.

"Like you, then?"

"Like me," said Melanie, "except Freddie is an editor. I am a humble feature writer."

At that moment, a man in a suit came in through the door, looked at Eddie and gave a crooked smile which revealed a gold tooth that caught the light. He looked like a gangster. I assumed this was his friend.

"Sorry, I have to go," said Eddie. Again, he shook my hand, said goodbye to Melanie, and then joined his friend at another table in the opposite corner of the restaurant.

The food was delivered and we both tucked into it. A thought nagged away at my mind. Not a thought, exactly; but an observation.

"He seems like a lovely chap," I said, not meaning a word.

"You mean Eddie," she replied. "Yes, very pleasant."

"You know him?"

"Barely."

"*Barely?* I'm surprised you know him at all. I know you love the sport and all that, but it isn't exactly the sort of circle you move in, is it? Your friends are more, how shall I put it, *well heeled.*" I wanted to look Melanie accusingly in the eye, but concentrated with studied attention at the patterned tablecloth in front of me.

"I met him backstage with Keiko when I researched the article. She was hanging around his dressing room door. We all got talking."

"Well, he has a good memory for names, then."

"Yes, he obviously does."

"As do you."

"As do I."

The meal arrived and we ate in silence. I was angry. He seemed to know her well... *too* well. He remembered her name and she remembered his. There was a familiarity between them that was more than casual. She was holding something back from me. I could sense it. As

I hate rows, I kept my suspicions to myself. I thought maybe I was being foolish. Maybe it was just the green-eyed monster. I let it drop. Her excuse was plausible, I suppose. And yet... I don't know. Something didn't ring true, but I didn't know what or why.

A week later, I went to pick up Melanie at the flat. She was in the shower. I sat down in the armchair. Keiko was lounging on the sofa with her head in *The Times* newspaper.

I said, "We bumped into a friend of yours the other night, a guy called Monahan."

"Edward," she beamed, peering over the top of her newspaper. "I haven't seen him for well over a year."

"I thought you were close friends."

"No. He is more Melanie's friend than mine. How is he, anyway?"

"He's fine. Sorry, I thought he was *your* friend?"

"Not really. I've met him twice, that's all. Why do you ask?"

"No reason."

"Are we ready to go?" said Melanie, as she came into the living room. "We are going to see a film today, aren't we?"

I got up from the armchair without answering. I was angry. Melanie had blatantly lied to me. She knew this guy pretty God damned well, knew him better than Keiko did, who had only met him twice.

I was pretty sure now Melanie had been a K1 groupie, and in all probability, still was one. I suddenly remembered the flock of girls whom she bumped into on her way out from the Ladies at the Royal Albert Hall. They were K1 groupies, I was sure of it. They were young and good looking... and they knew Melanie...because she was one of them!

This news shouldn't have surprised me. She found men who fight sexually exciting. She liked sex. She was friends with Keiko, who was, *is*, a K1 groupie. Melanie was a K1 groupie. She had fucked Eddie. That is how they knew one another. Everything added up.

For the past week, I had trouble focusing on my work. My mind had been racing with one thought: Had Melanie cheated on me? While we had been dating, had she fucked any of her beloved fighters? In short, had she betrayed me? My mind had seethed with anger, jealousy, and a desire to know the truth. Now I was certain I had the truth, my jealousy intensified and my anger swelled beneath the surface looking for release.

We drove to the West End in more-or-less silence, parked in a car park, and then walked to a cinema in Leicester Square. We sat in a foyer waiting for the film to start.

"Guess what?" I said. "It seems that Keiko knows Eddiewhatsisname as well."

"Oh, are you still dwelling on that. Yes, she knows him. How do you think *I* got to know him?" I looked at her and shrugged my shoulders. "She's a groupie," said Melanie, emphasising her words as if explaining to a dim child. "She knows a lot of UFC fighters. She gets to know them and I get to know them incidentally."

"Incidentally?"

"Yes. Incidentally. I think it was last year when there was an event at Wembley. She took me backstage, some of us had a drink with the fighters and one of the fighters there was Eddie."

"What happened then?"

"What do you think? They disappeared somewhere and I'm left with a wine glass whiling away the time while they have more fun than me. Is that a satisfactory explanation?"

"No," I said, disappointed with her blatant lying. "You see, when I was speaking to Keiko, I happened to mention we bumped into the incredibly fuckable Eddie and she told me that she had only met him a couple of times and that, *really*, he is a friend of yours. Shall I repeat: A friend of *yours*."

My voice must have risen because several people turned their heads away from their hot dogs and popcorn and gazed in our direction.

"Don't you speak to me in that manner and keep your voice down!" she snapped, her back arching and her eyes widening. However, I got the feeling her reaction was as much a defensive mechanism as anything. I saw a hint of panic in her eyes, like an animal that was trapped, ready to fight, but frightened at the same time.

"I'll speak to you how I damn well like!"

"Oh, fuck the film. I've lost interest. I'm leaving."

She got up and flounced out of the cinema. I followed a small way behind. We were making our way towards the car park. The streets were crowded, but at that moment, I felt very alone and very far from Melanie.

"You know, Freddie," she said, spinning around and looking at me directly in the eye, "you are being extremely stupid and unreasonable."

"Unreasonable? I don't see how. I am certainly not stupid. When we were in the restaurant, I could tell you knew Eddiewhatsisname *intimately*. He also knew you *intimately*. I am a little surprised."

"I do have friends outside journalism, you know."

"I can see that. Like Keiko, you have friends in the fight game."

"What is that suppose to mean?"

"You know fucking well what I mean! Keiko's taste in men is the same as yours. You probably share the same hobby." I stopped in the street and glared at her. "I don't get you. I really don't. What is it about you and men who fight? How far does your bloodlust run? I get the impression if we lived in some wretched country like Iran, you would be travelling all around the country to gawp at public executions."

She stared at me open-mouthed in amazement at what I had said.

"What? We share the same hobby! What is *that* supposed to mean?"

"You know what I mean."

"Oh, don't be so stupid! What about you? What floats your boat? What gets your end up? Well, I think we know, don't we. I bet if I *did* attend an execution, you would follow me just to get a rise out of my reaction." She pushed past me.

"Taxi!" she shouted. A passing taxi slowed down and stopped. Melanie turned to me and said, "I gotta dash off to Tyburn and see a hanging. God, you are such an idiot!" She climbed in to the taxi, said something to the driver, and the taxi drove off. The sound of its engine faded as it turned a corner and disappeared.

"Fuck!" I roared, to no one in particular, but turning the heads of passers-by.

Chapter 8

An Invitation to a Fucking

A cold war began between Melanie and me. I bumped into Keiko in the office — we were using a photograph she had taken for the magazine, — but we merely exchanged pleasantries. She obviously knew relations between Melanie and me had frosted over and she did not want to get involved.

For a week, Melanie and I did not speak. I was sure, *sure,* Melanie was a K1 groupie. The evidence was all there: She knew Eddie Monahan. She was friends with Keiko, who was a self proclaimed K1 groupie. When I read her article in *Raunch,* she fished around to find out what I thought of Keiko being a groupie. When I asked Melanie out-right if she was or had ever been a groupie herself, she became evasive. Any one of these things by themselves proved nothing, but put them together and they represent a pretty good case for the prosecution.

I spent that week brooding over her blatant betrayal of trust. I thought of her as a lying, deceiving little bitch. That is what I thought and that is how I felt.

Or did I?

I was betrayed. I had been lied to. That was undeniable. But I also felt... how can I put it, I also felt *excited* by the thought that she had been fucking all these fighters.

Probably... *maybe... hopefully...* she had sex with the fighters after being sexually aroused by watching them fight. That she had done it behind my back is a deceit, but it fed into my sexual desire. To be blunt: I found it a complete turn on. This is how she is and if this is why I am so attracted to her, I shouldn't moan when she behaves true to nature. I should rejoice.

I would like to say I thought this through in a moment of contemplation, when I approached the situation with logic and reason. Sadly, no. It was the reptilian part of my brain, my instinctive behavioural part of my grey matter, which saw through the dilemma of my situation: I am turned on by watching Melanie get sexually aroused by men fighting. But it is other men who are turning her on. Not me. Naturally, she desires to have sex with the men who arouse her. The thing that attracts me to her is the thing that makes me jealous; therefore, my jealousy is inappropriate.

It was while I was in bed, alone, when I started thinking about Melanie cheating on me, about her meeting up with Keiko, going to bouts behind my back, cheering on the fighters, getting sexually charged by the bloody spectacle taking place before her eyes, and then going backstage to complete her sexual desire.

As I conjured this scenario in my mind, my prick swelled and I found myself lying in the dark, slowly, but with a steady increase in my hand movement, masturbating.

I pictured both Melanie and Keiko watching with intense glee as fists and blood flew through the air. I imagined their pussies becoming increasingly moist.

Oh yes, yes. The movement of my hand became increasingly frantic.

Then afterwards they would consummate their sexual passion with fucking, or giving a blow job, to the men who were the objects of their sexual fantasies.

I ejaculated wildly, the spunk coming out in great spurts.

I let out a cry of joy, of release, realising immediately the cry of release had been Melanie's name. I slumped back in bed realising the contradiction in my jealousy of Melanie's unfaithfulness, that her behaviour was what I found most desirable in her. As I lay panting, I wished I had some paper handkerchiefs by the side of the bed. My sheets were covered with spunk. Fuck!

So there you have it. The thing that drove me away from Melanie was the thing that attracted me back to her. However, I could not suppress my natural jealousy. How could I reconcile these two opposites? Melanie and Keiko would resolve it for me.

Friday night, I got a call.

"Freddie, it's me." It was Melanie. She sounded tipsy.

"Melanie. How are you?"

"Fine. Keiko is here. Why don't you come over?"

I got in my car and drove over to the flat. Keiko let me in and then she slumped into the settee. On the other end sat Melanie, who was holding a half empty glass of wine.

"Would you like a drink?" Keiko asked. I nodded and she poured me a glass of wine. I sat down in the armchair wondering where this was going, wondering if this was an attempt at reconciliation, and wondering why Keiko was here. Surely, if Melanie was aiming at reconciliation, then Keiko would have discreetly retired to her own room and left us on her own. On the other hand, it was her flat, so she could do as she wished. They had obviously been getting drunk together.

Keiko slumped back into the settee, picked up a small magazine and, with a mischievous smile, handed it to me.

"What's this?" I said.

"A magazine," Keiko replied.

"I can see that," I snapped impatiently back. This reduced both girls to a fit of giggles.

"Turn to page 45," said Melanie.

The magazine was *Erogenous Erotica* which prints articles and stories about sex. I turned to page 45 and found an article entitled, "*Life As A K1 Groupie by Sylvia Taylor.*" It was accompanied by a photograph of a near naked K1 fighter with a totally naked blonde girl hanging off him. I looked up at Melanie.

"You're Sylvia Taylor, aren't you?" I said.

She nodded.

"I wrote this piece about six months ago. It's totally autobiographical. Read it to understand me and hopefully, you will understand. It explains me."

I started reading it:

What is your view of Cage Rage? A barbaric spectacle? An exciting contact sport? Or, if you are a woman, do you find it a bit of a turn on?

If you are in the last category, don't worry, you are not alone. An increasing number of women are turning to these matches and not all of them for the thrill of the sport. Some women find it explicitly sexual. Why?

So far, this article was a re-write of what she had written under her own name for Raunch. I continued reading. It was about two thirds of the way in that my interest was aroused. It differed from the original in the detail. It described the groupies who hung around fighters in the hope of getting laid. It interviewed and told the story of Stacy Oldham, an experienced groupie. The sex, far from being suggested, was vividly described in detail.

"A night that sticks in my mind," said Stacy, "was when Michael the Mad Mauler [name changed to protect his reputation] had just won a fight. Blood was smeared all over his muscular and sweaty body. I rushed backstage and met him. He stripped off and so did I. He lay on a bench and I climbed on top of him. We held each other tight and kissed. I felt his enormous cock stiffen beneath me." "Fuck me, baby," he groaned.

"Fuck me you little slut, you fucking trollop!"

"I rose up, spread my legs, and came down on him, his twitching cock sliding into my pussy. As his penis then slid all the way in, I felt an electrical charge surge through me and ....

It carried on and on in that tone.

When I reached the end of the article, I put the magazine down. Melanie and Keiko were next to each other on the settee opposite me with their knees drawn up to their chins, both clutching their glasses of wine. They both looked at me bleary eyed.

"So?" said Melanie.

"Well, I gather you interviewed yourself and that you are also Stacy, right?" Melanie nodded her head and smiled. "So you are a K1 groupie?"

"I was."

"Was?"

"I gave it up when I started going out with you."

"She used to have the same *hobby* as me," said Keiko.

"So I gather," I replied.

Keiko patted the space on the sofa in between the two of them.

"Why don't you sit down here with us?" As instructed, I rose up and then sat down between the two of them. Melanie took one arm and Keiko took the other and both girls cuddled up to me.

"Did you like the article, Freddie?" Melanie asked, and then ran her hand across my crotch. She reacted with delight when she noticed that it was slightly erect and started giggling. "You were right, Keiko, he did like the article."

To my great surprise, Keiko's hand stretched out and grabbed my cock. It got stiffer.

"You know what I said to Melanie before you came over?"

"That I would become aroused by the article," I replied. It was true. I found the whole thing completely arousing and the fact that Stacy was really Melanie gave it an added *umph*.

"Apart from Melanie's prettiness and cuteness, I know what you like about Melanie," said Keiko. "You like the fact that she is so sweet and still gets turned on by men fighting." I nodded. "So the fact that she fucks those very fighters she loves to watch fight should be an incredible turn on for you — and judging by the enormous growth of your cock, it is."

It was true, all of it, even the bit about the enormous growth of my cock.

"Darling," slurred Melanie, the wine really getting to her. "Just because I fuck fighters, doesn't mean I don't love you. All of us, the groupies, have steady boyfriends."

"Think of it as a hobby," added Keiko. "I think that was your word for it, wasn't it?"

I nodded.

"Yes, a hobby," slurred Melanie.

"When you next have a wank," said Keiko. "Just think of your so-pretty-pretty cutey-cute girlfriend fucking a blood smeared thug in a dressing room. You will reach orgasm in absolutely no time at all and you will love it."

They had obviously planned this meeting in advance and had played it their way from the very start. However, I didn't mind. They knew me; knew my desires. Understood my complex but animal attraction towards Melanie.

"We have a plan," said Keiko, unzipping my trousers while Melanie took out my fully erect cock.

"There is a Cage Rage event next month," said Melanie.

"We want to go," added Keiko.

"Yeah, we want to go and fuck some fighters," said Melanie.

"We are fighter fuckers," said Keiko.

"And I want *you* to watch *us* do it," said Melanie as she stroked my cock, which, under the handling of the two girls, had become enormous.

"I thought you had given up your hobby when you met me. At least, that's what you just said."

Melanie shrugged her shoulders.

"I want to fuck a fighter in front of you, just for you," she said, and then added mysteriously, "You're not going to deny me my hobby, are you?"

What could I do? I was helpless.

Melanie lowered her head over my cock and took it into her mouth. Her head bobbed, her lips sliding along my shaft, her tongue rolling around it. My cock twitched violently. Keiko asked how would I like to see Melanie being fucked by one fighter after another. I erupted with ferocity into Melanie's mouth. She pulled back and swallowed my cum down her throat. My head flopped back on the sofa. My breathing was ragged and exhausted.

Melanie threw back the contents of her wine glass down her throat, smiled at me, and said, "Shall we go to bed now?"

We got up from the sofa and to my surprise, all three of us trotted into Melanie's room, undressed, and then climbed under the covers. Luckily, Melanie had a large bed and we all fitted into it comfortably. I was in the middle.

Melanie fell asleep immediately but Keiko purred into my ear, "What was your answer? You never said."

"My answer is yes."

"Good. You will enjoy it. Melanie is a lovely girl, isn't she?"

"Yes, she is."

Keiko kissed me on the cheek, and then, astonishingly, brushed her hand over my cock. She smiled mysteriously, turned over so that her back was facing me, switched off the light and went to sleep. I lay there. I had just violently ejaculated, so it didn't stiffen much. But it did slightly. I stayed awake for about fifteen minutes in the dark. I could feel the heat of the two girls' bodies. I could hear their steady breathing. Thankfully, neither girl snored. I thought about Keiko's last gesture. What a surprise. What did it mean? I was to find out before the night was over.

An hour before dawn, I awoke to find Keiko stroking my swollen cock. It was dark, but there was enough light thrown in by the street lamp outside for me to see Keiko's smiling face. She pushed the duvet over so that it lay on top of Melanie, pushed me onto my back, slid over and silently straddled me. She lowered herself onto my cock. My erection slid into her moist vagina. She stifled a groan.

I looked sideways. Melanie's back was turned to me. Her breathing was regular and steady. Thank God she was asleep. I hoped against hope she would not wake up.

Grabbing hold of my shoulders, Keiko closed her eyes and started jerking her body up and down, increasing the pace of the rhythm with each jerk. I lay back and watched her small and soft breasts bounce rhythmically in time with one another. I watched her body sway above me. In the half-light, her skin tone and body took on a strange spectral look. I took a breast in each hand and fondled them with my fingers. The nipples stiffened to my touch. Her arms slid around my head and she pulled my face into one of her breasts. Relishing the warm milky flesh, I took her nipple in my mouth, and started gently to tease it with my tongue. My penis throbbed uncontrollably. I closed my eyes, and came.

I thrust my body up, bucking Keiko, making her lovely breasts bounce forcefully. I ejaculated and shot every last drop of spunk from me. I thought I had never felt such pleasure. As soon as this was done, she threw back her head, arched her back, and lost herself in a spectacular but silent orgasm.

When she had finished, she fell forward onto the bed, and buried her face in the pillow beside my head. Her ragged panting was loud in my ear.

"God, that was good," she whispered softly while slowly regaining her breath. She rolled over onto her back and lay beside me.

Melanie turned towards me, opened her eyes, and said with a wicked smile, "Did you enjoy that?" I didn't know what to say. "I bet you did and I bet you haven't got any spunk left for me." She felt for my prick which was limp and spent. "I knew it. Typical man. A woman can have a hundred orgasms in one night. A man, one, and that's if you're lucky."

Both girls laughed, cuddled up to me and fell back to sleep, as I did; but not before contemplating my increasingly complex relationship with Melanie... and Keiko. I began to think they were manipulating me, that they had a game plan, of which they had not informed me. Strange to say, I found that thought quite exciting. I was ready to go with the flow and see where it took me.

And what was it that I had agreed to? To watch Melanie (and Keiko?) fuck a fighter after a fight? How was *that* going to play out? It would all become clear very soon.

Chapter 9

Two Performances in One Night

Several months later, another K1 match took place, this time at the Wembley Conference Centre. I parked the car and the three of us joined the throng of people who were snaking their way towards the evening's event.

Melanie and Keiko looked stunning: Short skirts with high heeled shoes that emphasised their pert little bottoms. They both looked gorgeous and they knew it. They were blatantly flaunting their sexuality. Like female spectators at the Coliseum, they were out to catch the eyes and the attention of the gladiators. They were putting themselves on display and sending out the message that they were keen to get laid.

"You two look so hot that you're practically sizzling," I said. I meant it, too.

"Thanks," said Keiko, and then added with obvious authority, "We're dressed for a purpose."

So this was it. I was going to watch Melanie (and maybe Keiko) get fucked by a fighter. I was going to witness K1 Groupies in action and have a front row seat. I had an unsettling feeling when the girls went backstage, a muscle bound gorilla of a security guard would probably be less thrilled with my presence. I was curious to see how this was going to pan out.

The previous two months had been strange. After having sex with Keiko with Melanie's obvious approval, I had wondered how my relationships with Melanie and Keiko would develop.

The truth was it remained as before. I was Melanie's boyfriend. Keiko was Melanie's friend. I was Keiko's friend. It was as if nothing had happened that night. I thought about *that night* every day, especially as sex with Keiko was really good, although not better than with Melanie. Since the two girls lived together and I saw Melanie regularly, it was difficult not to see Keiko regularly as well.

When I dropped by, Keiko would treat me as she always had done, with a friendly *hi* and *how are you?* But nothing more. No conspiratorial winks. No nudges. Even when I saw Keiko alone, and occasionally I did, due to our jobs making our paths cross every once in a while, she never referred to the incident. It was strange.

Melanie was still the same with me. We got on well, had sex often, and the fact I found out she was a K1 groupie didn't really change a thing, it just made her even more sexier than before. I was beginning to realise now the more I got to know Melanie, the sexier she became.

We went through the entrance of the Wembley Conference Centre, showed our tickets, climbed the stairs, and went to the bar. I bought drinks for all of us. We sat down on a sofa by a vast window which overlooked the newly built Wembley Stadium.

"How's this going to work?" I asked.

"Wait and see," said Keiko. "Do you have your press card with you?"

I tapped my breast pocket.

"I have it."

"Good," she said. "Await further instructions."

"Melanie, we have to go," said Keiko.

Both girls rose.

"Take your seat and keep your phone on," said Melanie. "I'll ring you. Enjoy the fight."

"You enjoy the fight," I said.

"Oh, we will."

They tottered off balancing precariously on their high heel shoes.

By the time I had finished my pint, the bar and foyer area was crowded with people busily downing drinks and talking nosily. It was mostly men, but as always, there was a high proportion of women, some in large groups having a girls' night out and some in groups of two. I even spotted a few girls by themselves.

I took my seat in the auditorium. I was pretty high up and I had a good view. However, without Melanie by my side, Cage Rage held no interest for me. If anything, it felt meaningless.

I have never been a sports fan, least of all contact sports. I couldn't understand the mentality of the morons who took part. When a fighter wins a fight, he still gets beaten up, and sometimes badly. However, that wasn't why fighters fight. They actually loved participating in the sport. As deeply as I thought about it, I didn't get it. I couldn't get into a fighter's mindset.

People started to pour into the auditorium and the seats began to fill. The lights went down and the entertainment started. It was the usual nonsense and without Melanie by my side, I really did see it for the nonsense it was: Unadulterated hype.

The pumped up cheesy '80s power chords. The flashing lights. The over the top introduction by the announcer. It was pure show business, until the fights started, and then it got very serious. This was not World Wide Wrestling. This was not theatre. This was not just part-and-parcel of the entertainment industry. This was pure no-holds barred fighting. And the crowd, after having been hyped up, loved it.

I scanned the crowd for women, but was unsuccessful. Any woman who was there was sat elsewhere, annoyingly out of my view. I was a bit disappointed. But I held my phone in my hand ready for the call Melanie had promised. I was really intrigued as to how this night was going to turn out. My expectations were high. I was anticipating so much.

I kept my eye out for Melanie and Keiko and when the second fight came round, I saw them in the front row. I wondered how they got such good seats. Had someone reserved the seats for them, and if so, who? The fighters? Or maybe just *one* of the fighters?

They sat in the front row, intently watching the fights, cheering them on, getting excited when the action heated up. When the third fight came on, it suddenly came to me who in all likelihood got the seats for them: the man mountain himself, Eddie Monahan. This revelation came to me when the announcer boomed his name out loud.

Monahan strode down the ramp to a fanfare of Mötley Crüe's enduringly entitled "Mutherfucker of the Year". There was a dazzling display of lights, and he was flanked by flunkies and bikini clad girls. Melanie and Keiko rose to their feet and cheered and applauded as loudly as anyone. The applause around me was deafening.

I can't remember his opponent's name but in the second round he got knocked out and the crowd went crazy. I looked down at Melanie and Keiko and they were on their feet applauding and cheering. I wondered how else they were going to show him their appreciation.

After a speech filled with mind-numbing crowd pleasing banality, Eddie Monahan trotted back up the runway to a repeat blast of Mötley Crüe and accompanied by his entourage. I also noticed Melanie and Keiko getting out of their seats and wandering off. Were they going backstage to join Eddie? Five minutes later, I got a text message. It was from Melanie.

"Make your way to Level 2 entrance 4. Do you no where it is?" it said.

I texted back saying that I did and made my way there. I got to Level 2 entrance 4 and was met by Keiko.

"Come with me," and she led me through a corridor to a door that had an ape guarding it. "Follow me and show him your press card." She then turned to the ape and said, "He's with me. He's here to see Eddie."

I showed him my press card and he let me pass.

Keiko's words rebounded in my brain. *He's here to see Eddie.* I wondered if that was true and I thought it probably was.

I followed Keiko through another corridor that milled with countless other people until we arrived at a door. Keiko knocked. The door opened slightly. Keiko spoke her name, the door was flung wide open and she walked through. I followed. We were in a room where a number of men, about ten of them, sat around looking vaguely bored. One of them, a big man with a shaven head, jerked his head at another door. Keiko nodded, walked to the door and knocked. It was opened by Melanie. We walked in and Melanie closed it behind us, turning the lock. Finally, we were in the inner sanctum, or so it seemed to me. Christ, what a carry on! There were more doors being opened and shut than a West End farce!

"You must be Freddie," boomed out a voice I recognised instantly. I looked around and lying on a padded massage table, completely naked, was Eddie Monahan.

"Yes. We have met before. At the restaurant."

"Oh, yes. I remember."

"Congratulations on winning the fight" I said, a bit disconcerted that he was completely nude.

"Oh that. Thank you," he replied. "Did you enjoy it?"

"Yes. It had me gripped," I lied. "You're very good."

"Thank you," he said. "I understand you want to watch while your girlfriend gets, um, intimate with me."

I nodded.

"If you don't mind."

He threw back his head and roared with laughter, "No, I like people watching. I wouldn't let you do it otherwise. I'm not fucking stupid." He indicated a chair in the corner. "Sit down and make yourself comfortable. I hope you enjoy yourself."

"Thank you," I said, and sat down.

"Come on over," he said to Melanie, who complied by unzipping her dress in a swift movement and letting it slip to the floor. She was not wearing a bra. She then pulled down her panties. She leant down and undid her shoes and slipped them off. She stood naked before Eddie

"How do I look," she asked, giving Eddie a lingering simmering gaze, a sort of look that she never gave me.

"Fucking fantastic. Now how about coming over so I can have a good grope."

She strode over to him, her eyes never leaving his, her walk betraying just enough of a wiggle to be perceptible. Damn! She looked hot!

She climbed onto the bench, sat astride him, and started kissing him on the lips. He caressed her bottom and thighs. She then sat up, lifted up his arm, told him to clench his fist, and then started to kiss it and rub it against her body, especially her breasts. She closed her eyes and groaned, obviously relishing the feel of his fist on her naked flesh. She bent over and lowered her body over his face, sliding in a nipple between his lips, which he greedily started sucking. I could see his cock grow increasingly stiff and was now protruding up in between Melanie's buttocks. She rose up, slid down to his feet, and took his cock into her mouth. She started sliding her head back and forth like a piston.

I found the whole sight increasingly erotic, a fact betrayed by an increasingly growing erection. I felt a hand brush against it. I turned round and saw Keiko kneeling against me, looking up at me, and smiling.

"I can see you are enjoying the show," she said, and then turned around to Melanie and asked her, "Can I?"

Melanie took Eddie's cock out of her mouth, looked at us, and said, "Of course. Go ahead." She then put Eddie's cock back into her mouth and continued with her blow job.

Keiko unzipped my trousers, slid her hand in, and gently eased my cock out, which was now hard. Keiko put her head onto my lap, took my cock into her mouth, and started bobbing her head up and down. Both girls were doing the same thing, giving a man a blow job. I could feel her tongue tease my cock until it started twitching violently.

Before me, the sight of Melanie giving Eddie a blow job excited and thrilled me. Melanie withdrew her head; perched herself up on her hands, lifted her bottom up and gently lowered her vagina onto Eddie's quivering cock. She let out a groan as it slid inside her. He, too, let out a desperate sigh.

Keiko meanwhile pushed my legs apart and took my cock more firmly into her mouth. I could feel her wet lips slide up and down my cock and every now and then she would give me a soft bite, not hard, but just enough for me to feel it. God it was delicious.

But my eyes were satiated with the view of Melanie riding her fighter. She was bouncing up and down, her breasts bouncing in unison, her breath coming in ragged pants.

"Fuck me," she insisted, "Fuckmefuckmefuckme. Fuck me like you fucked up that cunt's face! Fuckmefuckme!"

"You fucking whore," he cried out. "I know what a slut like you wants." And with that, he arched his back, gave out a cry like a dying animal, and ejaculated.

"Yesyesyes!" she cried. "Oh God, yes!" and then she let out a piercing orgasmic cry, and her body shuddered as it came hard.

By this time, my cock was quivering and twitching like it had a life of its own, which it seemed to have. I no longer had any control over it. I could feel Keiko's lips sliding up and down my cock, her teasing tongue trying to wrap itself around my shaft. I let out a shout of delight and I came in Keiko's mouth. It came in spurts. Keiko sucked greedily and until every last drop of spunk had been extracted from my body. She pulled her head away, wiped her lips dry, and looked up at me.

"Did you enjoy?" she asked.

"I loved every moment of it," I panted, my breath coming back slowly by degrees. She stood up. Melanie was lying across Eddie's body.

"Come on," said Eddie to Melanie. "Get up. I got things to do."

Melanie got off Eddie and put her clothes back on. When she was dressed, she went over to Eddie and kissed him on the lips.

"That was great," she said, "and I loved the fight. I couldn't stand that creep. I wanted you to seriously hurt him, to make him suffer real bad."

He kissed her back.

"I will next time, baby, just for you. I'll give you a good show."

"I want to see it," she said, her eyes alive with expectation and stroking his massive arms. "Mash him up good. I want to see him suffer right in front of my eyes. I want to see his blood on your fists."

"I will baby, next time. Now you have to go. You all have to go."

On the journey home, the two girls sat in the back of the car. Over the steady reverberating hum of the engine, there was a silence that was almost beatific. The street lights overhead created a strobe like effect through the windows of the car. I felt I had to say something in order to break the spell.

"Did you enjoy yourself tonight?" I asked.

"Yeah, great," replied Melanie. "Did you enjoy *yourself?*"

I nodded.

"Yeah, it was great."

"Anyone going to ask me?" piped in Keiko.

"Did you like Freddie's cock?" asked Melanie.

"It was okay," she replied, causing us all to laugh.

"It's the best you've had tonight, at least," I said.

"I wouldn't necessarily say that," she said cryptically.

I smiled and looked at her in my rear view mirror. I saw Melanie and Keiko exchange knowing smiles. I wondered if Eddie was the only one Melanie had fucked that night. Probably not.

Afterwards, I had gone back to the bar and waited there by myself for over two hours. It was obvious I had only had a glimpse of that particular night's activities. I didn't think they would want to limit themselves to just fucking one fighter. The thought strangely pleased me.

Another thought strangely pleased me. I wasn't just having sex with my girlfriend; I was having sex with *her* friend, as well. Penetration two months ago. A blow-job two hours ago. I had a feeling I would be having sex with Keiko again, and probably soon.

Chapter 10

Melanie Asks a Pertinent Question

That night, I slept over with Melanie. We made love, despite being satiated by Keiko's blow job. It was a passionate bout of love making.

Melanie and I held each other's naked bodies tightly, her smooth skin and warm flesh pressed hard against mine. I ran my hands over her soft buttocks. My lips teased her nipples — easily the most sensitive part of her body — which made her groan in ecstasy.

I closed my eyes, relishing Melanie's body, and thinking of her having sex with a professional fighter and thinking of all the professional fighters she had fucked in the past. All these combined to make my cock hard. I plunged it hard into her vagina, thrusting past the swollen labial lips and into her wet cunt. The engorged head of my prick thrusting against her G-spot made her groans of ecstasy even more intense. I kept thrusting, thinking of Eddie thrusting, harder and harder. I came. Several thrusts and my spunk spurted out of me, copiously and gloriously. She came at the same time, her groans turning into screams.

"Fuck me! Fuck me!" she shouted. "Fuck me Eddie, Fuck me!" Her body arched and then was shaken by her orgasm until her body went limp. The last vestiges of her orgasm subsided and her cries of delight became an exhausted ragged panting.

I thought about what she had cried out during her orgasm. *Fuck me, Eddie, Fuck me!* I should have been consumed with jealousy, but I wasn't. Against my own interests, I found it an added excitement.

We lay there, not moving. I buried my face in her hair, her body beneath me. Her breathing had resumed a more regular and relaxed rhythm. Her breasts moved gently in time. Her hand carelessly played with my hair while her other arm was stretched out across the bed. My cock was now limp but was still inside Melanie.

"Baby, that was wonderful," said Melanie.

"I loved it, too," I replied.

She carried on running her hands through my hair.

"You didn't mind me shouting out Eddie's name, did you?"

"So you were thinking of him when you were making love to me?"

"Yes, but not when I was fucking him. I was thinking of him beating up his opponent during the fight."

"But you said: Fuck me. You didn't say: Beat him up."

"And when I was fucking Eddie, what do you assume was going through my mind?"

"Eddie beating his opponent up?"

"Exactly. Why do you think I wanted to fuck him in the first place?"

We lay there is silence. I thought about Eddie Monahan, about how she had made love to him and how she had called out *his* name while I was having sex with her

After a while she asked, "Did you get into fights at school?"

"A few."

Her eyes opened and a smile spread across her face. The light was off but the street light outside illuminated her quite clearly, even if her colour was blanched out.

"Go on," she said. "Tell me more."

"What is there to tell?"

"The fights. Did you win them? Tell me about the last fight you had at school."

"I was at sixth form at school. It was about four weeks before I left for college. Another boy, his name was Jeremy Taylor, jostled me in the corridor while we were on the way to classes. I told him to watch where he was going and that he was a fucking idiot."

"So you started it. Cool."

"Not really, well, sort of. He came up to me and asked if I wanted to take that back. I said no and told him to fuck off."

"So you fought him?"

"Yes. We agreed to meet by the sport's pavilion after school. All the fights took place behind the sport's pavilion because it was out of view from the teachers."

"Go on."

"Well, we met after school and there was a whole crowd there to watch it. So, we fought. He took a punch at me. I took a punch at him. Before we knew it, we were beating the living crap out of one another. It went on for about five minutes, but in the end, I won."

Without saying anything, she leant over and kissed me on the lips in the half light of the bedroom.

"Would you have cheered me on?" I asked.

"Of course. I used to like watching fights at school. I cheered on the boys I wanted to win."

"How did you decide which boys you wanted to win?"

"It would be either because he was a friend of mine, or because he was handsome, or at least handsomer than the other boy. Sometimes I didn't like one of the boys and I wanted to see him get beaten up."

"To see him get mashed up," I added.

She laughed.

"Yes, to see him get mashed up. I remember in High School, there used to be lots of fights. I think I watched them all. When I left school and went to college, the boys didn't seem to fight and I missed that, until I discovered K1. Oh, that was life changing. Real fights, just like in school, but with loud music and dazzling lights. Occasionally I saw fights outside nightclubs when they were closing and they were pretty cool, but I rarely went to nightclubs, so I didn't see *that* many."

"Kids nowadays form Fight Clubs," I said. "Would you have liked that?"

"God, yeah," she said. By this time, my cock, which was still in her vagina, had swollen. Listening to Melanie talk like this always did that to me. She noticed, smiled, and asked, "Again?"

I nodded. I started thrusting my hips faster and faster until I had built up quite a speed and then I ejaculated. There was not so much cum this time. But I enjoyed it and I think Melanie did too, although she did not have an orgasm.

We lay still for a few minutes and then I fell asleep. I presume she did too, because when I awoke the following morning, we were still in the same position. She was on her back with one arm spread out and her other arm around my shoulders. I lay on top of her, my face pressed against her right breast. Her steady rhythmic breathing told me that she was still asleep. I blew in her ear.

"Time to get up, darling," I said.

Twenty minutes later, I was sat at the breakfast table sipping my morning coffee. Keiko, putting marmalade on her toast, sat opposite me. Melanie, cracking open another egg, sat to the left of me.

I felt strange. Only last night, I had watched Melanie being fucked by another man while Keiko had given me a spectacular blow job. Later that night, I had fucked Melanie twice in a row. And now here I was, in a scene of domestic normality, having breakfast with both girls. Sometimes life is strange. Not that I was complaining. Strangeness can be fun. Life was good and I didn't want it to end. I considered myself incredibly lucky to have found two such girls as Melanie and Keiko.

"Guess what?" said Melanie, addressing Keiko.

"Yesterday, you got fucked by two men," replied Keiko mischievously.

"Maybe," replied Melanie, equally mischievously. *Maybe.* So it wasn't only Eddie and me who fucked her yesterday. I wondered which fighter other than Eddie fucked her? "But apart from that. Go on, guess."

"The Queen's abdicated."

"No."

"The Queen's been assassinated."

"No. What's this obsession with the Queen, anyway? No. Freddie and I were having a little chat in bed last night."

"Makes a nice change from sex."

"Oh we had sex all right." Melanie glanced my way and gave me a grin. I grinned back.

"Since you're curious," I said, "And you are a very curious woman, we had sex twice."

"And a blow job from me earlier on in the day. Now about the little *chat* you two randy love birds had in bed last night?"

"Freddie was telling me about the last fight he had."

"Was it recent," asked Keiko.

"No. It was not recent," said Melanie. "It was when he was at school in the sixth form."

"Did you win, Freddie?"

"Of course he did. Can you imagine Freddie fighting, Keiko?"

"Fighting me?"

"No, not you."

"I wouldn't dare," I added. "I'd be too frightened."

"Why don't you get into a fight for Melanie?" said Keiko. "You know how she would love that. Maybe we could arrange a fight with Eddie."

"Keiko. I would rather fight you and I'm terrified of you."

"Keiko. Don't tease. I'd hate to see Freddie get hurt in a fight."

"Ah, how sweet," simpered Keiko.

"I'll tell you what," I said. "I'm going to take a shower. While I do so, I'll let you two arrange a fight for me. Just make sure it's someone I can beat."

I went into the bathroom, disrobed, and stepped into the shower unit. As I stood beneath the shower, letting the water pour over me, I pondered over last night's conversation with Melanie and today's banter over the kitchen table.

Melanie asked me about my last fight and I told her. Why had she asked? Okay, knowing how it is with her, it is not so unusual she should ask such a question. But what did she think of my answer? Was she disappointed? Did she want to hear of a more recent fight? Did she secretly wish I was a bit of a brawler? She said at breakfast that she would hate to see me get hurt in a fight. But was that realistic coming from her? Wouldn't *me*, her boyfriend, getting into a fight, be a turn-on for her?

Why did Melanie bring up last night's conversation at the breakfast table? Was it to get Keiko involved in the discussion? Maybe they had discussed this already and had brought it up in order to get my mind working? It was certainly true that they tended to work together. Maybe Melanie and Keiko had engineered the conversation?

Maybe? Maybe? Maybe? So many questions. Maybe I was looking too deeply into things. How *were* their minds working? If at all.

I was in love with Melanie and I was sure that she was in love with me. Yet, she didn't mind if I fucked Keiko. Maybe Keiko is the sop she offers so she can fuck all her glamorous K1 fighters. Maybe—*Maybe*. That word again—*Maybe*.

Another fight came up and, of course, Melanie wanted to go.

"Just the two of us, this time," she said. *No Keiko?* "No Keiko. And no going backstage to fuck the fighters. I just want it to be the two of us."

This took me by surprise. She had got me used to the idea she wanted to go backstage to fuck the fighters and now she was making out that it was just another date. I asked where it was to take place: Wembley? Royal Albert Hall? York Hall?

"The Hope and Anchor in the East End of London."

"*A pub?*"

"Yes. It's in the basement, downstairs. It's not K1 as such. Oh, Freddie. How to explain it? It is like K1, but where as K1 still has to go by the rules, the fights in the Hope and Anchor don't, if you see what I mean?"

"They're illegal fights."

"Yes."

"How did you get to hear about it? Have you been to one before?"

"No, I haven't. Keiko knows the man who runs them. His name is Mitch. I've met him. He was at a Cage Rage event and Keiko introduced us. Every now and then our paths cross. Are you interested, because if you are, I may have a surprise for you."

"A surprise?"

"Yes, a surprise." She leant forward and kissed me on the lips. "A surprise once we are there."

"Okay," I said, intrigued. "I'm game."

What was her surprise going to be? As it turned out, it would be pretty intense. A step up, shall we say, in our symbiotic relationship.

Chapter 11

The Fucking Room

On the night of the fight, I collected Melanie from her flat and drove across London to the slums of the East End. We went down Shoreditch High Street, a street of grubby Victorian buildings that consists mainly of Bangladeshi owned shops, past a grimy strip club which looked as if it had seen better days, past Brick Lane with its plethora of Indian restaurants, and past a dilapidated Valence Road, childhood home of the notorious Kray twins, gangsters who terrorised London during the 1960s.

I was feeling apprehensive. The area was vibrant, foreign, and decaying. With the night falling, it exuded an air of menace. This was not the most salubrious part of London and I was anxious for my safety, Melanie's safety, and the safety of my car. Where were we going to leave it and would it be safe?

"Turn left here," said Melanie. I turned left into a dimly lit street. "Turn right here." I turned right and found myself driving into an abandoned allotment surrounded by a ring fence. There were several cars here, some nice ones, as well. A Mercedes. A Rolls. A Jaguar. A tough looking man in a black suit directed me into a space.

"You 'ere for the fight?" he shouted. I nodded.

"Are all these cars here for the fight?" I asked Melanie.

She nodded and smiled.

"Are you excited?" I said I was. She grabbed my arm, squeezed it and said, "It's going to be so thrilling. You're going to love it."

We got out the car, and with Melanie leading, who after all, knew the way, walked out the car park and up the road. Melanie hooked up with me and I could feel her shivering. There was a cold wind. The street was deserted. My anxiety at the unfamiliar surroundings made me alert. I also became aware of Melanie's vulnerability in this less than salubrious area.

She looked gorgeous. She wore an expensive looking fur coat. I wondered what she wore underneath. She wore red high heel shoes, which was an indicator she was dressed to the nines, which meant she was more than likely wearing a sexy little number. I wondered if that was wise. This was neither Wembley nor the Royal Albert Hall. This was a rough part of London, the East End, to be exact, which carried with it a reputation of street gangs and violence.

We carried on walking, her high heeled shoes going clippity-clop, clippity-clop, like a horse. My eyes were everywhere, looking out for trouble.

"Here we are," she said. We stood outside an old pub. The hanging sign read "The Hope and Anchor." We walked in. The pub was empty apart from a few customers scattered around. By the ease with which they held themselves, I guessed they were regulars.

Melanie went to the bar and handed a bartender a ticket. He looked at it, then at Melanie, then at me. He jerked his head and we followed him around to the back of the bar, down a narrow corridor, through a door and down a rickety old staircase without a carpet. Once we were downstairs, there was another door, through which I could hear a low murmur of voices. In front of the door stood a man very similar to the one in the car park: Tough looking and dressed in a black suit. He wore an ear-piece with a wire disappearing down into his collar.

"They're 'ere for the fight," said the bartender. Without saying a word, the doorman opened the door and indicated with a jerk of his head that we should go inside. We walked in. The goon closed the door behind us.

Before us stood a crowd of what must have been about sixty — maybe more — people. They looked at us as we entered and then went back to their own business. There was quite an assortment here. Groups of young men in suits: City types. Older men with hard faces and mean eyes, also wearing suits: Villains. Melanie was not the only girl here and we were not the only couple.

Because it was cold, all the girls had coats on, but they were unbuttoned. Most wore short skirts with plummeting cleavages. There was a fair amount of sparkling jewellery hanging from ears or strung around necks. Melanie unbuttoned her fur coat and I saw her short red dress.

"I see you're not wearing a bra," I said, with a smile. I could tell because her nipples were outlined by the fabric of her dress. I love it when she dressed like that. What man doesn't like it when his girl dresses sexily?

"I'm not wearing any knickers, either," she said teasingly. I liked the way she dressed even more. "I want to look like a tart tonight. Come on. Let's get a closer look."

We moved into the front of the crowd. Before us stood a ring fence that blocked off one end of the basement.

"I guess this is where the fight takes place," I said, stating the obvious.

"I guess," said Melanie, smiling.

Curiously, on the wall at the back of the basement, in the area where the fights, presumably, took place, was a long mirror that stretched right along the wall. I gazed through the chicken wire at my own reflection gazing back at me.

"So when does the entertainment start?" I asked.

Melanie replied by cuddling up to me.

"I'm cold," she said. I put my arm around her and pulled her close. "There are six fights tonight," she added. "They should be starting soon. The first fight we shall watch from here."

I looked at her in surprise.

"And where are we going to watch the second fight—from the back of the hall? From the roof, maybe?"

She smiled and put her finger on my mouth to hush me.

"No, silly," she said. "You'll see. Don't worry. You'll like it when I take you there."

"There? Where's there?"

"Don't be impatient. You'll find out soon enough." Melanie was talking in riddles. And, if what she was saying was true, why wasn't she wearing knickers? Not for the first time with Melanie, my mind was bubbling over with intrigue.

At that moment, a large man in a dinner jacket strode through the crowd followed by the two men stripped to the waist and wearing only shorts. When they reached the chicken wire, the dinner jacket opened a door in the ring fence and ushered them in. He then closed the door.

"Ladies an' Gen'lemen," announced the man in the dinner jacket in a booming cockney accent.

The main lights had gone off, leaving only a single naked light bulb hanging above the caged in area. There was a hint of expectation in the air.

"For your entertainment, we 'ave the first fight of the night. In the left 'and corner, we 'ave Buster Bates from Margate."

There was a round of applause from the crowd.

"And in the left 'and corner, we 'ave Barry "the Gypsy" O'Connell."

There was a loud roar of applause and shouts of "Go on, Barry." He was obviously a local lad and his fans were here. The referee indicated the two fighters to step into the middle of the cage, which they did.

"Okay lads. You know the rules. No eye gouging and that is the rules. We want a good dirty fight."

There was a titter of laughter at this throughout the crowd.

"And it is not over until I say it is. My instructions must be obeyed at all times." They nodded. "Let the fight begin," said the referee and he stood back and leaned against the wall.

Melanie held tightly on to my arm and I caught her face in the mirror that stretched out across the opposite wall. Her expression was one of expectation. I could tell by the faint hint of a smile on her pretty face that she was anticipating a violent and bloody fight. God! She is so sexy when she is like this. This is Melanie at her very best. I felt a faint stirring in my loins. Thank God it was dark in the auditorium. I could hide my erection from other people.

There was a roar from the crowd as the fight erupted in a flurry of fists and the two fighters forced each other one way and then another. I could see Melanie's face smiling callously, but as she did so, her hand grabbed hold of my cock and pulled it several times. God! That felt good. She let go and moved in front of me. I put my arms around her waist and rested my jaw on her head. I kissed her behind the ear. She forced her bottom against my crotch. I pressed forward. My erect cock rubbed against the cheeks of her arse, which she wiggled discreetly but provocatively, and my erection swelled.

The fight grew even more intense as the crowd cheered and egged them on.

Then one got the better of the other, and pummelling his face with his fists, opened a cut above his eye. His face became a mask of blood. The crowd got excited, including Melanie. I could tell by the way her body stiffened. Cries of "Kill him!" and "Finish him off!" filled the room. One voice pierced the air, "Go on! Mash him up!" This last outburst was from my sweet and lovely Melanie.

I looked around the crowd and all eyes, wide with delight and alight with expectation, were fixed intently on the fight. This was it. The kill.

As the loser collapsed under the rain of punches, the referee stepped in and pulled the victor off. Just as well. If he had continued, he would have killed him. The loser looked well and truly *mashed up*. The crowd erupted into applause and cheers for the winner. So did Melanie, who jumped up and down with burning, cruel elation.

"Wasn't that great?" she exclaimed gleefully, taking hold of my arm and squeezing it gently. She then looked me in the eye, discreetly brushed her hand softly against my erection, which was still raging, and added, "This is pretty great, too." She kissed me gently on the lips. "After we have calmed this monster down a bit," she said, indicating my cock, "I intend to take you somewhere else to watch the next fight."

After a short while, my cock softened and I no longer had to hide it.

"It's okay, "I said. "It's decided to take a nap. I can walk without having an enormous tent bellowing out in front of me."

"That's a shame. I quite like the idea of that," she said. She hooked up with my arm and led me away from the milling crowd towards, to my great surprise, a door at the back I hadn't noticed. Melanie knocked on it. It was opened by the large man wearing the dinner jacket. It was the referee.

"Hello Mitch," said Melanie.

"'Ello, sweetheart," said Mitch. "Come 'ere for the private room, 'ave you?"

"Of course," said Melanie. "May I introduce you to Freddie, my boyfriend?"

"'Ello, son," said Mitch, taking hold of my hand and shaking it vigorously. "You two love birds follow me." *Love birds?* Where was he taking us? We followed him through a corridor, through another door, and into a darkened room. "I'll leave you two in peace. There's no lock, but I promise you won't be disturbed. Have a good time."

With that, he left the room with us in the semi-darkness. When I say

71

semi-darkness, there was no internal light in the room itself, but light did flood in through the window which looked out on to the fight arena, from which we had just come. It was a massive window which took up nearly the whole of the wall. I was amazed. Then it struck me. The mirror in the arena was not an ordinary mirror: it was a two way mirror. We could see them but no-one in that room could see us. I thought this so odd. I had no idea why we were left alone for a private, no, a *secret* viewing of the fight.

Melanie turned round, faced me, and then let her coat slip to the floor, so that she stood only in her red dress.

"What do you think?" she asked.

"What do I think? Why the private room? Why not watch out there where there is, at least, more of an atmosphere?"

"You know, Freddie, for an editor of a magazine, you are a little slow on the uptake sometimes," and with that, she undid the back of her dress and let it slip to the floor. She stood before me naked, apart from her high heeled shoes. "Now do you understand?"

"Oh God," I exclaimed in amazement. "You don't mean..."

"Yes. That is what this room is for... to enjoy ourselves while we watch the fight." She strode over to me, put her arms around my neck, kissed me on the lips, and added, "Some people like champagne while watching a fight, some a meal; but we prefer something else, don't we, darling?"

I kissed her on her lips and then stood back. Following Melanie's cue, I quickly shuffled out of my clothes. We both stood naked in front of the two way mirror. There was an electric heater in the room, but I still shivered. It felt strange. It was like standing naked in a crowded room. I knew they couldn't see us, but I couldn't shake off the feeling that they could. I also felt that someone might walk in at any moment. There was also a leather couch in the room in front of the two way mirror. I stood behind Melanie, held her around the waist and we watched the second fight.

It was another gore fest which excited Melanie. Each time she screamed with delight, I ran my hand over her flat stomach and down over her freshly shaven pubic mound, or sliding over her breasts, needling her nipples until they were as erect as my cock had become, all the while kissing her on the neck. Every now and then her hand would slide behind her, and even while her eyes were fully on the fight, she would stroke my cock, making it harder and harder until it was rock hard and waiting for some action.

"This fight is good, isn't it?" sighed Melanie. I grunted a yes. "Wait until the next fight, then I'll be ready."

When the fight had finished and the bloody winner stood over an even bloodier loser, my cock was twitching as if it had a life of its own, which, in part, I suppose it did. I had to stand back because every time it twitched against the soft round buttocks of Melanie, it would be in danger of exploding.

Melanie saw what I was doing, looked admiringly at my cock, and said, "You're ready. So am I. Don't worry honey, the next fight will soon be on, and I hear it's going to be really something."

The third fight quickly followed. The two fighters laid into one another with blood curdling violence.

Melanie's eyes widened with delight, looked at me and said, "Okay, now. Do it to me, now." She knelt on the sofa, her legs apart and her cunt on display. She gripped the back of the sofa and levelled her eyes on the bloody spectacle in front of her. I stood behind staring at the round globes of her buttocks and thrust my twitching manhood into her vagina, sliding past her swollen labial lips, into her incredibly moist and dripping wet pussy, — God, had she been turned on by this evening's entertainment — and I started thrusting back and forth, back and forth, making her groan.

Then she shouted out, "Fuck me, harder! Harder! Please! I want to be fucked hard, oh God, yes, fuck me hard!"

My buttocks went back and forth more and more rapidly until I came, my spunk spurting into her cunt with the force of a tidal wave. At that moment, one fighter felled the other with a punch to the mouth that sent blood spaying across the mirror.

"Oh yes! Lovely!" she cried out and came. Her body shook. She arched her back and then let out a loud orgasmic scream as she closed her eyes, for once taking her view off the blood fest before her, and allowed her body to be over-whelmed by her orgasm.

I pulled back, shivering in the cold, and we both stood up. The two fighters left the arena and Mitch wiped the blood off the mirror with a rag, smiling knowingly through his own reflection at us. We both got dressed and then left, not bothering to see the other fights. She had got from them what she wanted. So had I. On the journey home, we said nothing.

We slept in Melanie's bed. We didn't have sex. I didn't have anything left in me. My body was spent. Melanie fell asleep as soon as her head hit the pillow. I lay there thinking about tonight. There is no doubt about it: Knowing Melanie has made my life so much more interesting. If I had never met her, life would have been that much duller. Tonight proved it.

At breakfast the following morning, questions had been in my head all night were still circulating. I had to ask.

"Melanie," I said. "About last night."

"Did you enjoy it?" she asked as she cracked open the top of her egg with a tea spoon.

"Yes, it was wonderful, but..."

"Where did you go?" asked Keiko. This really was becoming a three way relationship.

"Hope and Anchor," replied Melanie.

"Oh, so you went, did you?" replied Keiko. "How was it?"

"Excellent as always," replied Melanie.

"It is a strange place," I said, "what with the two way mirror and everything."

"Oh that," said Keiko. "That was originally put in to film illegal fights surreptitiously. I met Mitch at a Cage Rage event two years ago and he told me about it."

"You remember Mitch, darling" added Melanie. "He was the man who let us into the room last night."

"Well," continued Keiko. "I met him backstage. He's friends with some of the fighters and I fell into conversation with him when he told me about this room he keeps under his pub. He runs the Hope and Anchor. The basement has illegal fights nearly every month. He buys the police off and that is why he's never been raided. At least, that's what he told me.

"I asked if he filmed every fight. No way, he said, just some. So one night he gave me a ticket for a fight and he took me into the room with the two way mirror, and sure enough, we watched the fights in that room. It was after the first fight that the idea came to me. Hire the room out to couples, I said, so they can, how should I put it, enjoy themselves while watching the fight."

"We call it the Fucking Room," piped in Melanie, "and the other room is called the Fighting Room. The Fighting Room and The Fucking Room. Cool, isn't it?"

"Did you fuck Mitch while watching the fight?" I asked.

"What? Fuck Mitch? No way. Besides, he's not turned on by that sort of thing. I had to explain that some people are and he could make some extra money by doing that."

"How much for a session? " I asked.

"Two hundred and fifty pounds."

I turned to Melanie and said, "You paid two hundred and fifty pounds for last night?"

"No, she didn't," piped in Keiko. "She got it for free. Because I gave Mitch the idea, he gives me permission to use it free whenever I want to. I rang him the other night and asked him if he would let you two use it. He obliged."

"Do many people pay to use the room?" I asked, genuinely intrigued.

"Yes. He doesn't exactly advertise it on the internet, but word gets around by mouth. You'd be surprised. It's not just us who have, how shall we say, this particular interest in sex."

This threw a new light on Keiko. I knew she got turned on by fighting, but I hadn't realised, until now, that like Melanie, she liked to be fucked while watching a fight. Keiko and Melanie have so much in common with one another.

I turned to Melanie.

"I don't know why you don't write an article about this place. For a journalist like you and considering the sort of magazine you write for, this is a Godsend."

"You are joking," snapped Melanie. "Mitch has connections to organised crime. No way am I going to cross him. Anyway, I like the place. I may want to use it again. In fact, I may want to use it soon."

With that she gently tapped my leg with her foot and smiled mischievously at me. I smiled back. I liked the place as well. I wondered how soon?

Chapter 12

A Suggestion

The following Sunday morning, we lay in bed. I had awoken early and made us both coffee, which I brought into the bedroom. The sunlight streamed through the net curtains. It was a relaxed lazy morning. Any moment soon, we would hear the Sunday papers sliding through the letter box and land with a dull thud on the mat. Melanie lay awake, but with her eyes closed. I climbed back into bed and ran my hands through her soft brown hair.

"Darling," I said.

"Darling," she replied without moving.

"I've been thinking. It's a wonder that you like me. After all, I'm pretty nerdish compared to the guys you like to watch fight and then fuck in K1."

"You have other qualities," she said, opening both eyes and propping herself up with her arm. "I like loyalty, kindness, wit, conversation. You give me all these things. I also like a nice cuddle, a good fuck, and excellent cunnilingus. You give me those things, as well. You see, as boyfriends go, you're pretty good."

"But still, don't you sometimes wish you had a complete brute that picks fights, someone who would excite you?"

She kissed me on the cheek.

"No," she said, smiling affectionately. "I want someone like you, for all the reasons I have just outlined. If I wanted a brute, I would have got one. As you discovered for yourself, I can get a brute any time I want. I have K1 for that, and that's enough. Do I really want a stupid thug for a boy friend? No." She kissed me again, as if to confirm what she had just said, or to offer comfort.

"What's brought all this on?"

I purred like a cat, appreciating the attention.

"Nothing, really. I was just thinking aloud. But still," I added. "How would you like to see me in a fight?"

She looked at me with a puzzled look on her face.

"You? In a fight?" I nodded. "Okay. You in a fight? It depends on the circumstances. I don't see you as a fighter, though."

"But would you like it?"

"Like what?"

"To see me in a fight."

"Do you want to get into a fight?"

"Answer the question."

"Okay. I suppose it would be cool."

"But would you enjoy watching me fight?"

"I suppose so."

"So you would."

"Okay. Yes. So, are you going to get in to a fight? Why? To please me?"

"Of course."

"Are you serious?"

"Of course."

She buried her face into the pillow and laughed.

"Tell me more," she asked. "Where is this conversation going?"

"I want to get into an organised fight. Just one. You must understand I don't want to make a career out of it. I just want to get into one organised fight and I want you, and hopefully Keiko, to watch the fight."

"And then to fuck you afterwards?"

"Yes."

"And for Keiko to fuck you, as well?"

"Not necessarily. I want *you* to fuck me." Actually, I wanted both of them to fuck me, and I don't think Melanie would have minded, but I couldn't say that for certain. I felt I could sell this idea better if I gave Melanie exclusive rights to my dick.

"Okay," she said, chewing her bottom lip while she thought this one through. She then swung her legs out of bed and said, "Let's get up." She put on her dressing gown and walked out into the living room.

By the time I joined her at the dining table, Keiko was already up. I sat down and poured myself a coffee.

"Keiko," said Melanie. "Freddie raised something while we were in bed this morning." We all collapsed into sniggers at that. "No, he raised *that* last night. He raised something else this morning."

"A flag of surrender?" said Keiko.

"I raised that ages ago," I said.

"He raised a suggestion," said Melanie, "Or to put it more succinctly, a desire he wishes to carry out. Freddie wants to get into a fight, an organised fight, and he wants me to watch. Well, not only me, you as well. Afterwards, he wants to fuck me."

We all lapsed into silence as we let the thought sink into Keiko's brain. She responded by raising her eyebrows and nodding her head, as if in contemplation.

"I see," she finally said. "What has bought this on?"

A good question. What had brought this on? Had I taken leave of my senses? Did I want to get myself killed? What was I letting myself into? Did I really stand a chance in an organised fight? I began to question my sanity.

Keiko, of course, answered her own question.

"You want to impress Melanie, to turn her on?"

"Yes, I want to turn her on."

"He wants to fuck me afterwards," said Melanie.

"But you get fucked by proper K1 fighters anyway." said Keiko.

"I know, but *I* want to fuck her after *I* have fought."

"So it is all about you?"

"It's about Melanie and me."

"And what do you think about all this?" said Keiko, turning to Melanie.

"I don't know," she said. "It came out of the blue while we were lying in bed. I just don't want to see Freddie hurt."

"But how would you feel if he won?"

"Quite excited I guess."

"So how are you going to get involved in this arranged fight?" asked Keiko.

"I don't know. I really don't. I was wondering if maybe you might have a suggestion — or maybe you and Melanie might be able to arrange something through your contacts."

Melanie and Keiko looked at one another and then back to me.

"You want us to arrange this fight for you?" asked Keiko.

"Yes," I said. "You two seem to know the fight scene. I don't. What about your boyfriend, James? He's a boxer. Doesn't he know someone who can arrange for me to get involved in a fight?"

There was a moment's silence, and then Keiko said, "James and I broke up. However, I think I can arrange something." Melanie and I gazed at Keiko. "But you will have to get into training."

"How do I do that?" I asked.

"Join a gym, of course, and learn how to box."

So I did. I joined Terrys Gym, without the apostrophe.

Before I even stepped into the gym, I had to buy boxing shorts, boxing boots, a head guard, a gum shield, and a groin guard. Once I had got all the accoutrements of boxing, I was ready to start my training. I was taking my first step in the world of organised illegal fighting.

Terrys Gym was in Covent Garden, which was handy for my office. I went three times a week. On my first evening there, I met Terry himself. Terry was a man in his mid thirties and an ex-boxer. For a boxer, he was surprisingly polite. Maybe unfairly, I always imagined boxers to be thugs. Why else become a boxer unless it is for the opportunity to beat someone up on a regular basis? So to find an ex-boxer who came over as amiable and kind was rather a surprise.

He was, as you would imagine, quite knowledgeable on the craft of fighting and gave me advice on all sorts of things I would never have imagined. For instance: his advice on boxing gloves. Do you think boxing gloves are just boxing gloves? No.

"When you see professional boxing," Terry explained to me, "You see gloves tied on with laces, which provides a nice snug fit for the boxers. However, when you are training in the gym, most gloves have Velcro wrist straps. This makes it easier to put the gloves on and remove them yourself. With boxing gloves that are laced, you need someone to put them on and take them off. The right size gloves are important as well. They come in small, medium and large sizes. The weight of boxing gloves can be anything from 10 to 20 ounces, and the heavier the glove, the more protection it offers."

However, before I got into the ring, I was given a series of exercises which included skipping, punching a bag, and shadow boxing, all of which thoroughly exhausted me. I also had to run five miles every morning.

I didn't go into the ring until my third evening there. Terry helped me on with the hand-wraps, which were there to provide extra protection for the knuckles, and then I slid on my gloves, fastening the Velcro nervously. I was to have my first sparring match.

"Sparring is *it*," said Terry. "If you are frightened of getting hit, sparring will remove this barrier. In fighting, that's all fear is, you know; the fear of being hit. Fear is a mental block. Nothing more."

I can't say it was too great being hit, but I kept my composure and did everything Terry told me to do. I used my right hand to protect my jaw and jabbed with my left. I learnt ring strategies. I kept moving left and right, threw straight punches, all the time looking for openings so I could use an uppercut. I learnt to keep the pressure up, to bob and weave and slip one under the jab. I circled the ring in both directions. On Terry's insistence, I practiced my jabs continuously as the jab is the most important punch in boxing, and to not let my right hand drop when throwing it.

Melanie and Keiko were eager to know every detail of my training regime, and to account for every bruise on my body. As I told them, they would first examine and then prod the bruise. I simply wanted Keiko to tell me when I was going to fight. Tired of waiting, I asked her.

"You know Mark?" Keiko replied. It was a rhetorical question. Of course I knew Mark. He was Keiko's new boyfriend. He was a lecturer at London University. Melanie and I were surprised at her choice of boyfriend. Keiko always dated fighters, but Mark, we assumed, was different. I met him a couple of times. I found him dry, academic, slightly nervous, and shy. Why had Keiko brought up Mark's name in this conversation?

Keiko noticed the confusion on our faces, smiled, and said, "Do either of you know how I met Mark?" We both shook our heads. "I met him at the Hope and Anchor."

"The Hope and Anchor," I repeated. "*The* Hope and Anchor?" She nodded. "He was a customer?"

She shook her head. "No. He was taking part in a bout."

Both Melanie and I looked at Keiko open-eyed in surprise.

"Mark!" exclaimed Melanie. "You're having us on, right?"

Keiko shook her head.

"You don't understand Mark. Although he seems shy and nervous, he does throw a great left hook. He's an excellent fighter. So much so that when I saw him fight at the Hope and Anchor, I really wanted to fuck him, so I did. I took him to the Fucking Room, we fucked, and it was great. I kissed the bruises all over his body. I kissed his blistered and bleeding knuckles. And when we finally did it, it was fantastic. You really must try him one day, Melanie."

"So looks are deceptive?" I said. Who would have guessed it? Shy nervous college type a fully paid up member of Fight Club.

"This is fascinating," I said. "But it still doesn't answer my question."

"I think she has," said Melanie.

I gazed directly at Keiko and said incredulously, "You mean I am to fight Mark?"

She nodded. "At the Hope and Anchor."

I nodded. "When?"

"Three weeks time. Sunday the fourteenth. It will be in front of an audience. The winner gets three hundred pounds. The loser, nothing. Are you ready for it?" I nodded. "Good. May the best man win."

Melanie put her arms around my neck and kissed me on the lips. "Darling. I'm sure that the best man is you."

For the next three weeks, I went to the gym every evening. I got up early every morning for my five mile run, came home and did my exercises. I stuck doggedly to the diet given to me by my trainer, Terry. I had told Terry that I was anxious and nervous, but he gave me endless advice and encouragement. Melanie also gave me endless encouragement.

"I'm so proud of you darling. I'm sure you will win." She would cuddle up to me in bed, rub her hand over my body, and say, "Mmmm, the taut body of a fighter. I can't wait to see it in action." We made love every night. "You know. There seems to be a glow about you nowadays." To be truthful, there was a glow about *her*, a wide-eyed, dazzling smile demeanour about her whenever she looked at me. I knew what it was. She was eagerly anticipating the fight. I could see her, yelling at me through the bars to *Mash him up! Mash him up!* This is what I wanted. To arouse her blood lust. For me to be the object of that blood lust arousal. This was my sexual fantasy come to life. And I milked it for all that it was worth.

"Are you looking forward to the fight, my love?" I asked, taking her in my arms and kissing her on the lips, and getting a full kiss in return.

"I really want to see you fight. I know you will be magnificent in there. I'm sure you will beat Mark."

"How much do you want me to *beat* Mark?"

She purred. "I want you to beat him hard."

"Mash him up?"

"Yes, really, really mash him up." Her eyes were alight and her mouth curved into a smile. She kissed me again and held me around the waist, one hand sliding down to my left buttock.

"Do you want me to finish him off quickly for you... or slowly?"

"Slowly. Very slowly. Yes, that would be delicious."

Delicious.

"I'll savage him in front of you, so be right in the front, right up close, where you can see everything," I said, sliding my tongue in between her lips.

"Yes, yes," she said, thrusting her hips, her cunt, against my groin and easing my prick, which was now swollen, inside her. "I'd love that. Please do it."

"I hope you have a strong stomach because he is going to be a bloody messy pulp. Blood will be everywhere and...."

And before I could finish the sentence, she pushed me onto my back and my prick slid out of her vagina. She, disappeared beneath the duvet, took hold of my throbbing cock, slid it into her mouth, and began sucking it greedily. Her head began bobbing up and down as my cock slid in and out of her mouth. I felt ready to come at any moment. I threw back my head and closed my eyes ready for the spectacular ejaculation. I could feel it building up in my loins, like an oil strike ready to blow. At that moment, Melanie rose up and straddled my cock.

Her cunt thrust down on my swollen prick. She was wet and it slid in between her labial lips. As she took a firm grip of my shoulders, her body started bobbing up and down with increasing rapidity, up and down, harder and harder, until I could take no more, and I erupted inside the woman I loved.

She arched her back, closed her eyes, cried, "Yes, God! I want you to mash him up! I want to see blood! I want to see him in pain! I want it all. I want you to fucking kill him!" Then, her body convulsing, she let out a scream, and she came.

I slumped back on the bed and Melanie curled over me. Her breathing was ragged and her eyes were closed.

I whispered in her ear, "So you're looking forward to seeing me fight."

She opened her eyes, looked at me, and then smiled.

"Yes," and then added, "But I don't want to see you hurt."

Chapter 13

My First Fight

Several weeks before the night of the fight, Mark came to the flat to pick up Keiko. All four of us stood in the living room. I eyed him up, really, for the first time. Sure, he looked nerdy, but there was a steeliness about him. His nervous manner and steel framed glasses gave him his wimpish air, but strip him down to his waist, and I could imagine you would find a well-toned body. If his face appeared ineffectual, then his stance did not. He stood facing you, not turned slightly away in the manner of shy people. There was more to Mark than I had originally thought. I could imagine him being a formidable fighter in a ring, and according to Keiko, he was. This, after all, was Keiko's attraction to him. There was something of the Clark Kent/Superman split about him.

"I gather we are to fight," he said, plainly and without any hint of a threat. He could have said that we are to meet for a game of chess with the same easy detachment.

"Yes, we are."

"I understand that you've not fought before."

"I haven't."

"I'm sure you'll do fine. I've fought quite a few times now and I haven't won them all."

"That's very gracious of you," I said. It was, too. "But I'm sure you will be one hell of a formidable opponent."

"I assure you, I will."

We both smiled at one another, shook hands, and then he parted with Keiko.

"I got a feeling it's going to be a tough fight," I said.

"You'll murder him," said Melanie, with more enthusiasm than I, at least, felt.

I was beginning to have serious misgivings about this up-and-coming fight. What am I saying? I'd been having misgivings about this fight ever since I was rash, *stupid,* enough to put forward the idea. However, the sparring sessions in the gym were coming along fine, even though my body, especially my arms, ached like mad. Maybe, just maybe, I could win this. It was like being a kid again, getting ready for a fight after school. Yes, I kept telling myself, I can win this, while behind me my self-confidence was being nibbled away by self-doubt.

The night of the fight came.

I drove through the East End of London and parked in the same car park where I parked before. Melanie was sat beside me. I was not in the mood for conversation and Melanie, sensing it, remained silent. A gorilla in a suit, the same one as before, pointed out a place for me to park, which I duly did.

We got out. The sky was dark and the air chilly. We made our way to the Hope and Anchor. This time I was wearing a track suit. We got to the pub, went through the door and to the bar.

"You're Freddie deFord, right?" said the barman. I nodded. "Hang on, Mitch will want to have a word with you."

He disappeared down the stairs and came back up with Mitch right behind him. Mitch beamed at me.

"'Ello, son. 'Ow are you? You all right?" I nodded that I was fine. "Good, good, good. Follow me, I'll take you down. 'Ow are you, Mel, you okay, darling?"

"I'm fine," she said, and followed us as we went behind the bar, down the stairs, past the security and through the door into the basement. It was as before. The end of the basement caged off with chicken wire and the (two-way) mirror on the wall. In front of the chicken wire, people were milling around. Groups of men talked intensely about the up and coming fights, women waited expectantly, couples... *couples?* Why couples?

Is *this* where you bring a date? Of course you do. What are they going to do after the fight? It was obvious: they are going to fuck. Chances are it was the girl's idea to come to this fight.

Undoubtedly, there are some girls here who are mere trophies to show off the men. You can tell who. The men with expensive suits and diamond studs in their ears. Their aftershave reeking of illegality, of criminality, of shady deals, stolen goods, of fences. Their girlfriends know it, but don't care. They want the money, the clothes, the expensive gifts, and the exclusive clubs, which goes with being a criminal's girlfriend.

But even they, afterwards, will want to fuck; because even they, or very often, more than most, *they* will enjoy the spectacle taking place before them. They will be sexually aroused and they will want their sexual needs seen to.

Melanie nudged me.

"Over there," she said, jerking her head to a corner of the basement. I looked over and there were Keiko and Mark. They both smiled at us and we smiled back. Just at that moment, Mitch spoke.

"I understand you're going to fight Mark Dawes." I nodded. "Well, good luck. If this is your first fight, 'e's a good one to start with. Your fight with 'im is the first one tonight. I'll take you to the changing room."

I kissed Melanie and then followed Mitch. He took me through the door that led to his office. Inside there were two other doors. One led to the Fucking Room while the other led into a small room with a bench down the middle, a row of lockers against the wall, and a shower.

"This is the changing room," said Mitch. "Get undressed and I'll come in an' get you when it's your time."

I smiled and said thank you. He left and a couple of minutes later, Mark came in.

"Hi," he said, smiling. "You ready for tonight?" I nodded. "Good. Me, too."

We got dressed into what were really swimming trunks. I had been right about Mark. His body was incredibly firm and well-toned. His arms were muscular. Stripped of his clothes and steel framed glasses, he lost his awkwardness and appeared confident and assertive. Almost naked, he was a different man. I could see what Keiko so admired about him.

We were barefoot and we paced up and down the room like a couple of hungry lions, not speaking, averting eye contact, and psyching ourselves up ready for the fight.

My mind was racing and my heart was thumping away like a jackhammer. I had trained like mad and I kept Terry's advice in my mind.

Stay focused. Keep your mind on the fight. Don't rush in and try and get it over and done with. If you do that, it'll be over in a flash – with you on the floor, unconscious. Take your time. Get a measure of him. Size him up. Once you have done that, you will have worked out how he fights, and once you have done that, you will know how to defeat him.

The door opened and Mitch walked in.

"You're both on. Follow me."

We followed him through the audience and into the basement. There was only one light: a naked light bulb above the fight area, although I felt more naked than any light bulb. There was now a large crowd and all eyes were on us. One person started clapping and then everyone else joined in. We shuffled through the cage door which Mitch closed behind us.

"Ladies and gen'lemen," he announced. "The first fight tonight is between Mark Dawes," There was a loud cheer, applause and stamping of feet, "and Freddie deFord." There was more applause, this time a little subdued, and no cheering or stamping of feet.

I looked over at Melanie. She was stood right in the front, but she seemed subdued. I smiled at her and she smiled back. Keiko was right beside her. I hoped Mark and I would give the ladies an enjoyable entertainment for tonight. In fact, that was my sole purpose for being there. If I won the fight tonight, it would be such a turn-on for Melanie. I imagined what the sex would be like afterwards. *A super nova exploding in the centre of my universe.* Like nothing I had so far experienced.

"You know the rules," said Mitch. "There ain't no rules." There was a murmur of laughter from the crowd. "Except you stop when, and if, I tell you to stop, and no eye gouging. Let the fight begin."

He stood back. Mark rushed towards me and I briefly saw his fist fly towards my face.

I woke up in the changing room.

I was lying on the bench.

Standing over me was Mark, Mitch, Melanie and Keiko. I groaned. My jaw hurt like fuck.

"What happened?" I mumbled. I genuinely couldn't remember.

"You got knocked out by Mark," said Mitch. It suddenly came back. Yes, I had been knocked out by Mark. I could remember his fist flying towards my face. I had been knocked out by Mark within the first five seconds of the fight, and that includes the four seconds before Mark threw the first punch. I wanted to crawl into a hole. The humiliation was unbearable.

That night, after I dropped off Melanie, I went straight home. Everyone was very good about it.

Mark patted me on the back and said, "Don't worry. It's your first fight. It happens to us all."

"You did well, bruv," Mitch said. "Don't worry son, you did well."

"You were very brave," Melanie said.

After the fight, I had been swamped with kindness.

The truth was: I sucked. I didn't get fucked that night, either.

That night I lay back in bed and couldn't get to sleep no matter how hard I tried. I took aspirin to kill the pain in my jaw, but it was not that which kept me up all night. I ran the fight, all five seconds of it, through my head over and over again. By two o'clock, I got up, went to my living room, put on my headphones, and played a CD for distraction. But the image of that fist flying into my face would not go away. The music was just a background noise. After all my training, how could I have let that happen? What would I tell Terry?

I wanted another fight.

You want what?" said Melanie, the following morning. I had telephoned to run it past her.

"I want another fight," I repeated. "Put Keiko on. I want to arrange it through her."

Keiko came on the phone.

"Hi, Freddie. How are you? How's the face this morning?"

"It throbs and is heavily bruised." It was, too. What would I say to everyone in the office? I was due there a few hours later. "Keiko. Can you arrange another fight for me?"

"Another fight?"

"Yes."

"Okay. I'll ask Mitch, but if he says yes, it won't be until next month."

"That's okay. I can put in more training."

"I'll call you when I've done it. Melanie wants to speak to you."

"Darling, are you sure you want to do this?" said Melanie.

"Yes. I'm sure. I really want to do it."

"You're not doing this to impress me, are you? I don't care about last night. I just don't want to see you hurt again."

Yes, yes, it is all about trying to impress you. I want to get you excited. I want you to watch me fight, to be impressed by me, like you are impressed when you watch those gorillas that fight in K1. Through sheer physical violence and the spilling of blood, I want to make your pussy moist. I want to have that effect on you. I want to fuck you after that fight and for you to come with the same intensity as when you fucked Eddie Monahan. Melanie, my darling, my sweet sadistic darling, it is all about you.

"Of course it's not about you, darling," I lied over the phone. "It's about me. It's about me proving to myself I can stay in a fight for more than five seconds without getting knocked down. Wouldn't you like to see me do that?"

"Of course I'd love that," she said. See, she would *love that.* "But I don't want to see you get hurt again."

"Don't worry about me," I said with false bravado, "worry about the guy whom I am going to pulverise." She laughed at that. "Look, I'll come over tonight, if that's all right by you. I'll see you about eight."

I came over at eight and we fucked. It wasn't because she saw me fight last night, but because I was going to fight again. I had proved my courage and that excited her, I'm sure. On the other hand, it may have been a sympathy fuck, one for the poor cat.

Keiko got in contact with Mitch and arranged the fight.

The following month, I was back behind the wire fencing, and to my surprise, I was to fight Mark again. Mitch stepped back after he announced the fight had begun. The crowd went silent and I saw Melanie looking apprehensively at me. She was such a sweetheart that she didn't want to see me get hurt. She raised the subject several times during the past month.

"You don't have to do it, you know?"

"I know I don't, but I do need to prove this to myself." Then I would inevitably give away my real reasons for wanting to fight. "But wouldn't you like to see me fight? You like to watch those guys in K1. Why, you even fuck them. Watch me fight and then fuck me."

"You idiot. You're not them. That they fight is all I like about them, but I like you for you, for who you are. We can talk and laugh together. We like the same books and films and music. I like men who fight because I find them such a turn on, but I don't think about sex all the time, not even most of the time. It's great that you don't mind me fucking professional fighters, but that doesn't mean you have to become one."

"But I want to fight." There I go, trying to impress the sexual side of Melanie.

"But I don't want to see you getting hurt."

"Don't worry. I won't. You'll see."

I stood, for the second time, facing Mark, and his fist flew towards me as quick as last time, but I was ready for it. I jerked my body to one side, let the arm fly by me, grabbed it, pulled Mark towards me, and threw a punch into Mark's face. He recoiled back, but grabbed hold of my arm and pulled me to the ground. We both collapsed onto the rubber matted floor. I got in a punch to the stomach and he got a punch to my face. I felt blood in my mouth. My lip was cut. He hit me again in the face, this time in the eye. I jumped up onto my feet and kicked his still prostrate body several times. He grabbed hold of my leg and pulled. I tumbled down on top of him and he hit me on the jaw. I rolled back and he jumped up at me.

The crowd was roaring their approval.

I rolled over and Mark went tumbling to the ground on the spot where I had been. I rolled on top of him and started pummelling him with my fists. He tried to defend himself with his arms, but to no avail. The crowd roared me on. Mark slammed his arm twice on the mat, the sign for surrender. I leapt off him and jumped around like a clown, waving my fists in the air. I had won!

I saw Melanie. She was clapping and her face was smiling.

Mitch came over, lifted my arm into the air and announced me the winner. Everyone applauded. Mark got up, his face covered in bruises I had given him, and a drop of blood dribbled out of the side of his mouth. We embraced.

"Good fight, man," he said with extreme generosity. "Good fucking fight. You were awesome."

Yes, I was. I felt great. I felt alive. I felt horny. I wanted to fuck Melanie there and then. We stepped out of the fighting area. Melanie came over and embraced me and then gave me a great big sloppy kiss on the lips.

"Darling, you were wonderful."

She kissed me again, our tongues darting in and out of each other's mouth. We were horny as hell. I wanted to fuck her and she wanted to fuck me.

"Let's fuck," she said.

"Where? Here?"

"You know where." She dragged me off to the Fucking Room. As she shut the door, she undid her blouse and pulled down her skirt, unhooked her bra and pulled down her knickers. She left on her high heeled shoes. "Let's do it, now."

"I'm covered in sweat and blood," I said.

"I know," she said, walking up and embracing me. "I love a man fucking me when he is covered in sweat and blood."

I was cut on the lip and blood was smeared over my mouth. Melanie dipped her finger into the blood and then wrote a large M on my chest.

"M," I said. "What does the M stand for?"

"What do you think it stands for, silly?"

She dipped her finger into the blood again and then completed the word.

I now had the word *Melanie* written across my chest in blood.

She smiled at her handiwork and then kissed me on the mouth, smearing blood on her lips. She then went down on her knees and pulled down my trunks. She put my limp cock into her mouth, grabbed hold of my buttocks and started sucking. My prick swelled. As I gazed out of the mirror, another fight had just started.

Melanie got up and said, "Sit on the sofa." The leather sofa was against the mirror. I did as she asked and then she sat astride me, holding on to my shoulders with both arms, and let her pussy down on top of my aching cock. I knew what she wanted to do. She wanted to fuck while a fight was taking place behind me. She now had my cock in her pussy and her eyes on the fight in the next room. Her body went up and down, my cock twitching.

She kept mumbling into my ear, "You were wonderful out there. I wanted you to really mash him up. Oh God, you were fantastic. I loved it. Fucking loved it, oh God, yes, fuckfuckfuck me you fucking animal!"

God, she was hot. I felt my passion rise in time with my blood engorged prick. I wanted her now. I wanted to fuck her. I deserved her. I had fought. I had won. She was mine by rights. I had won her. I had won her body. Her petit, but well formed, feminine, sexy lusty body.

Her back arched, she threw back her head, and, as an orgasm soared through her body, she let out a piercing scream I thought would shatter the mirror. In that instant, I also came. Our bodies jerked rhythmically. I came in a torrent. I caught my breath and then let it go.

Our bodies went limp. Her head rested on my shoulder, her breath coming in pants.

"Fantastic," she said, her breathing ragged, and then she slid off me. "The best sex ever."

It was, too. I loved it. I loved fighting in front of Melanie. I loved Melanie. I loved having sex with Melanie directly after a fight. Damn it, this was the best moment of my life.

I went back to the changing room, leaving Melanie to get back into her clothes. Mark and Keiko were there. They gave me a knowing smile. They knew what had just gone down. As soon as Melanie came out, buttoning up her blouse, Keiko grabbed hold of Mark's hand and led him into the Fucking Room. I wondered how many more people were going to use that room tonight.

I showered, washing Melanie's bloody name off my chest, got dressed, and then we both went into the auditorium.

We waited for Keiko and Mark when a voice said, "Freddie. How are you?"

I looked up, surprised. I didn't quite recognise him at first, but there was something familiar about the face. He was a tall man with blonde hair and quite handsome. It came back to me. Eddie Wallis. A fellow journalist. He worked for one of the broadsheets. I had met him a couple of times and knew him to speak to. I was startled to find him here.

"Eddie," I replied, feeling a little embarrassed. He must have seen me fight. *Oh God! Is my little hobby going to do the rounds in the media village, a village that thrives on gossip?* "How are you?" I said, feigning pleasure at meeting him. "May I introduce you to Melanie?" Melanie and Eddie smiled at one another and exchanged greetings. There followed an awkward silence. "Did you see the fight," I asked, in order to break the silence.

"Yes. Very good. You made quick work with him."

"Do you come here often?"

"No. not really. I tell you what, why don't we go upstairs. I need a drink."

We went upstairs and sat by ourselves in a corner. The bar was almost empty apart from a few regulars chatting softly to the barman. The cigarette stained wood-panelling seemed to soak up whatever light there was.

Eddie sipped his beer, leant forward and said in a conspiratorial whisper, "I'm working undercover."

"Undercover?" I repeated. Melanie and I leaned closer to Eddie.

"That's right. Undercover. I'm doing an article about the world of underground boxing and that's why I am here. I was amazed when I saw you walk in. My article is going to be published in next month's issue."

I remained silent. I really didn't know what to say.

"Eddie," Melanie said, putting a hand on his wrist. "Could you not tell anyone that you saw Freddie fight? I mean don't mention his name in the article. Don't tell anyone in your office. Don't tell your friends. Don't tell anyone. If word gets out, people may get the wrong idea. You know what people are like."

Eddie vigorously shook his head.

"Of course," he said. "I won't say a word to anyone and I won't mention your name in the article, which is only about the underground scene generally."

"Do you know Melanie has written a piece about girls who attend boxing?" I said.

He looked at Melanie and said, "Are you Melanie Matthews?" She smiled and said yes. "I came across your article while I was doing my research. Didn't it appear in *Raunch*?"

"Yes," she said. "I'm on their staff."

"Yes, it was a very good article." He gazed at her in a strange way, and then added. "A very original take, if I may say so. Are you *undercover*, too?"

"No, I'm here to support my man," she said, snuggling up to me.

We chatted on and then Keiko and Mark came up.

"Here they are," I said. "I think it's time for us to be going home."

Eddie stood up and said, "It was great meeting you and of course, I won't say a word to anyone."

"I look forward to reading your article. Since Melanie and you are covering related ground, why don't you give Eddie your number," I said, turning to Melanie," and maybe Melanie can offer some advice."

"Sure," said Melanie, smiling at Eddie. "I'd be happy to be of help."

That night, I drove us all home: me, Melanie, Keiko, and Mark. I told everyone about Eddie Wallis.

Keiko sounded anxious.

"I am not happy," she said.

"Me neither," said Melanie. "The last thing we want is to have some journalist snooping around. What if the article publishes the name of the venue? It would bring the police into it. You know these things are illegal. What if they raid the place when we're there?"

"I know," I said. "I feel the same way that you do. However, he does have your number and I did say you would be happy to talk things over, so… why not have a chat with him, see if he is going to name the venue, and if he is, try and talk him out of it."

"What if he doesn't ring?" said Melanie.

"Then ring him."

When we arrived at the flat, Mark went into Keiko's room and I went into Melanie's. I fucked Melanie again and could hear the sounds of fucking from Keiko's room. Oh yes, it was a great night. A night of unforgettable ecstasy. However, there was that nagging concern about Eddie Wallis and his article.

Chapter 14

School Days

Work was proving to be a problem. Not so much the work itself, but my appearance at the work place. Despite being editor, I did not have an office to myself. I shared it with fifteen other members of staff. My office was the top floor of a Georgian building. My desk was against a window that over looked Central London. I was very much on display, which I liked. Being in the middle of things meant I was accessible and I knew at all times what was going on. However, being on display did have its drawbacks, especially when you are black and blue from the night before.

After my first fight, when I had been so unceremoniously knocked out by Mark in the opening seconds (Seconds out, indeed!), I turned up at work with a swollen eye. The previous night, it had been black. The following morning it was black, purple and several other colours I couldn't put a name to. In short, I looked awful. Siobhan, my secretary, was the first person to comment on it.

"What happened to your eye? Have you been in a fight?"

"Training last night," I said. I told everybody I was sparring at the gym, but added it was purely to keep myself in shape. No-one had any idea of my illegal fighting life. Throughout the day, others commented. The weekly editorial meeting, which consists of six others, began with everyone staring in silence at my eye.

I smiled indulgently and said, "Before anyone asks, I spar in a gym several times a week and this is how I got my shiner. It serves me right for not wearing a head guard."

This seemed to satisfy most people, although who knows what was said behind my back. I began to get a little paranoid about this. What *were* they saying: *Has he been in a fight? Did his girlfriend give it to him? Did his girl friend's boyfriend lay into him?* These imagined quotations from conversations I was not privy to, or may not have even taken place, rumbled around my head for about the same amount of time my multi-coloured eye remained in place, which was about a week. I could have been upfront about everything, I suppose:

Listen, everyone. I took part in an illegal fight. It's a brutal pastime, certainly; but I did it to sexual arouse my girlfriend.

I could just imagine how well that would go down. I work for the sort of magazine that employs rather leftist types, and this blatant sexuality, this unabashed worship of masculinity, this sexualisation of violence, would be seen as the worst possible example of machismo.

What they would not understand is how Melanie is calling all the shots. Why would they understand? Hell, I don't understand it myself. My feelings on this subject, as are hers, are perverse, but none the less real for that. We are not acting out a role as one does in a fetish club. We are carrying out our desires for real and desires do not lie.

What lay at the root of my fantasy? I had been having these fantasies ever since I was old enough to masturbate. I knew my sexual desire was very unusual. Even the porn industry did not cater for it. There were magazines that catered for every perverse taste: bondage, masochism, sadism, sado-masochism, bestiality, and others, worse and rightly illegal. For Christ's sake, you can even get magazines full of old women! What the fuck is that all about?

But there is nothing—Nothing!—for men with my particular taste. I did wonder if my sexual desire was unique. I continued thinking it was unique until I was sixteen and my parents went on the internet. Eventually, I would find there were others like me, with *my* tastes, *my* desires. There was even an internet forum where we could talk about our particular fondness for a *certain* kind of girl.

God alone knows where this desire came from: why should my brain find this, of all things, so desirable? I do remember an incident when I was about fourteen.

I was walking home from school. I was alone. I took a short cut through a copse. Several larger kids appeared in front of me. I could tell by their blue blazers they were from St Joseph's, who, for some stupid reason, was a rival of our school.

I looked up. There were four of them; two boys and two girls. The boys stood side by side blocking my path. The girls stood behind them, grouped together, looking at me with suppressed smiles on their faces. I thought them pretty, but my attention was on the two boys, who also looked at me, but with anything but a smile on their faces.

I stopped. I had to. Either that or turn around and run back. In normal circumstance, I would have done so. There was no-one from my school to report my cowardice. Luckily, as it turned out, I didn't run.

"'Scuse me," I said.

"What the fuck did you say, cunt?" snorted one of the gorillas. I stood there, gazing hopelessly up at them, my face expressionless, not daring to say another word just in case it was the wrong word. I had a bad *bad* feeling about this. "I said, what the fuck did you say, cunt?"

He was several inches bigger than me, fairly fat, and had a mop of ginger hair. He grabbed me by my blazer lapels and pulled me close to him, so that his screwed up aggressive face was inches away from my frightened one.

I still said nothing. I was terrified. He pushed me away from him, let go of my lapels, pulled back his fist and then let it fly hard in the face. I flew back onto the grass, my jaw throbbing uncontrollably. The two boys loomed over me, saying nothing. Then the other one kicked me several times in the ribs. The one who punched me bent over and started slapping me around the head.

"You going to do something about this, you cunt?" he said. Cunt was his favourite word, evidently. It does have a certain bluntness and threatening finality about it.

"Leave me alone," I muttered. I was almost on the point of tears.

"Leave you alone?" he said. "What about it, girls?"

He turned around and looked at the girls. They stood there, silent and expectant, a look of affected disinterest on both their lovely faces. I was hoping they would take pity on me. They didn't. They shrugged.

"You said we were going to see a fight," said one of them.

"We haven't seen one yet," said the other.

I was doomed. These two bitches were going to be the ruin of me. And yet... my heart was pounding. These girls were beautiful. Even in my perilous state, I had noticed that, and not only beautiful, but sexy. And I had not only noticed that despite my perilous state, but because of it... and I realised it even then.

One of the boys, the one who had not hit me, said, "Well, what about it. Do you want to fight?"

"We can beat you up here and now if you want?" snarled Ginger.

One of the girls stifled a laugh.

I should have been whimpering, begging for mercy. Instead, I replied, with a slight tremor to my voice.

"Ok. I'll fight. Let me stand up. But I'll only fight one of you."

Out of the corner of my eye, I saw the two girls look at one another. This is what they wanted to see and I was going to give it to them.

"Whoa," said the boy who didn't hit me. "I have a new found respect for you."

They stood back and allowed me to stand up. I took off my blazer and laid it on the ground. The boy who hit me took off his blazer and handed it to one of the girls. She took it and neatly folded it over her arm. We squared up to one another.

I thought it would be over in a minute, with me lying flat on the ground. Defeated and humiliated before the girls. But no, it didn't go like that. Ginger held up his fists and threw some wild punches, which I easily avoided. I threw some punches which missed. Then I threw a swift one which made contact on the side of his face and then another one in the jaw that pushed him back. He jabbed wildly, but none made contact. I threw a few more punches that failed to make contact and then threw a hard right hook that did make contact and sent him flying to the ground.

As he fell, I caught a glimpse of the two girls. They were wide eyed, taking it all in, and relishing it. This was better than they thought it would be. I didn't want to disappoint.

I jumped on top of him and started pummelling him. He put up an arm to protect his face and with his free hand, grabbed hold of my shirt, and pulled me off, hurtling me to the ground. He rose on all fours and threw himself on top of me. My God! How quickly the tables turned. It was his turn to start pummelling me.

I was now flat on my back, with him sitting astride me, and throwing one blow at my head after another. I put up my arms to try and shield my face from the onslaught. I suddenly thrust out with my right fist, punching through a gap between his fists, and hit his face directly in the nose. It started bleeding profusely.

"Fuck!" he said, with anguish. "It's going all over my shirt."

Like I cared. It was, too. Blood also dripped all over me, as well. He got up, got out a handkerchief, held it up to his nose and tipped back his head.

"You all right, Derek?" said his friend.

"No, of course I'm not all right. My fucking nose is bleeding."

I got up off the ground, and not taking my eyes off the two boys, hesitantly put my blazer back on. I walked past them and past the two girls, who were studying me with renewed interest. Yes, I had impressed them! I gave a slight smile and one of them gave me a smile back.

"We are not finished, Cunt!" shouted my opponent, glaring at me malevolently. "This will continue at another time."

I gave a non-committal nod as if I didn't really care. I had, after all, won the fight. But it had been a fluke. He was no great fighter, full of bluster and show, but he was bigger than me and if I had not got that lucky punch in and bloodied his nose, I would have got stomped.

However, I had enjoyed it. I had fought bravely and willingly, despite nervousness, and it was all because I had an audience of two pretty girls whom I wanted to impress. And after the fight, one of them had smiled at me.

I had a throbbing jaw which would bruise. It hurt like mad. But, God! Yes! It had been worth it.

I went home and once in my bedroom, I locked the door and started to wank furiously, thinking of my fighting skill and how it had impressed those two girls. I fantasised how after the fight, I had sex with them, while the loser looked on, the girls humiliating and laughing at him. I made love to one girl and then to the other. After that, these two girls, especially *the one who smiled at me*, became my most treasured wank fantasy.

The following day, I went home by another route. I knew if I met up with them again, there would be another fight, and I might not be so lucky this time. Also, if the two girls were not there, I would have no-one to spur me on.

So even early on, all the indicators to my sexual desires were there.

It would not be long before my little problem arose, my inability to have sex with women. My impotency. Wanking, yes: I could cum in a minute. Sex with a woman: no, nothing would happen. It would harden and then, before performing, go limp, to my utter dismay.

Only Melanie made me cum. She was the woman who dissolved my impotency, gave me a sex life by fulfilling my sexual desire, however perverse or odd that desire may seem.

By fighting, by going into the cage, I hoped I fulfilled Melanie's sexual desire, too. I had *proved* myself to her. I had shown her I was a *man,* as much a man as any fighter she fucked. I could have ended my fighting career there and then. But no. The sexual high was too good, too much of a thrill. I also felt that it was in fact a drug which neither of us could wean ourselves off. It was incredibly potent, a sort of perverse Viagra.

This is how I felt, and although I cannot speak for Melanie, I was sure she felt the same. I felt we were plugged into a weird sort of national grid. Unplug us and our sexual desires would wither and die, and with it, our relationship.

So I decided to keep on fighting on the illegal circuit, probably at the Hope and Anchor. Melanie would always be in attendance, of course. There would be no point in me fighting if she wasn't. There were also other girls in the audience and I loved fighting in front of them.

However, my victory over Mark gave me a false confidence, as would become only too apparent.

Chapter 15
Meeting the Masher

The article appeared in the *Times*. "*The illegal world of East End Underground Fighting by Edward Wallis.*" I read it thoroughly, as did Melanie and Keiko. It mentioned the Hope and Anchor, but by another name. Melanie had met Eddie Wallis for dinner and discussed the article. He had said he was not going to mention the name of the venue, but I was worried that he, or maybe his editor, might go ahead anyway and print the name and location of the bloody place. But he didn't. We all let out a sigh of relief.

"Let's hope the police don't take an interest," said Keiko, voicing our fears.

Every month at the Hope and Anchor, I would fight. I was never a major attraction. The punters came to see others more capable; so I would be the first on the card. After my victory over Mark, I had a confidence I had never felt before. I had fought, and more than that, fought in front of my beloved Melanie — and won!

I walked with a spring to my step. I walked tall. I looked men in the eye and didn't back down. Oh, I realise I am going a little over the top here, but for me it was a big thing. Sex with Melanie was always good, but it just seemed to get better and I swear it happened more often than it once did.

My third fight took place the following month. Melanie and Keiko were pressed against the chicken wire, their fingers clinging through the holes. They were expectant, hopeful, and wanted to see a swift and glorious victory.

My opponent was a gypsy called Dave "the Masher" something-or-rather — I didn't quite catch his last name. As soon as the name "Masher" was announced, I began to have serious doubts. He was young and new to the fight scene; but his body was taut and muscular and he carried himself with the confidence of a man born to fight. He was going to work himself to the top of the illegal fight game from the bottom — and I was the bottom.

"Right," said Mitch. "Shall we get started? You know the rules. No eye-gouging and you follow my instructions. Otherwise, there are no rules. Now, let's fight!"

He stood back and I squared up to the gypsy who just gazed arrogantly at me as if I was beneath him. He also had a distinctive smirk on his face. This got me angry and worried at the same time. I put my fists up and jabbed at him. He weaved and ducked without actually moving his feet from the ground. I thought, *One good punch and I can knock this arrogant piece of shit to the floor for the count and wipe off his smirk for good.*

"Come on, Dave," someone shouted from the crowd. "'It 'im, for Chrissakesakes, will ye."

To my astonishment, Dave the Masher answered back.

"In good time, Pa."

I saw Melanie and Keiko peering through the chicken wire. The sight of them propelled me into action. I jabbed a few more times with my left and then followed it up with a swift hard right. Dave stepped out the way and then followed it with a right of his own that hit me on the side of the head. I felt, rather than saw, a couple more blows, then I collapsed onto the ground.

Dave jumped onto my prostrate body and started to hit my head. I put up my arms to protect me but several blows still got through. It was over. I was pinned down and defenceless. I banged on the floor in submission.

To the roars of the crowd, Dave jumped off me and started punching the air with his fist. He then nonchalantly walked through the door of the wire cage and swaggered off to the dressing room.

Mitch helped me to my feet.

"You all right, son?" he said, lifting me up under my arms and hoisting me to my feet.

"I'm fine," I said, which I was, apart from the pain.

"A round of applause for the defeated," shouted Mitch to the audience, who dutifully, and probably sympathetically, obliged.

I walked out of the cage and Melanie stepped forward and kissed me on the cheek. The *cheek*, mind; not the lips.

"Never mind, darling, you were wonderful in there," she said, without any conviction at all.

Keiko gave a wistful smile and said, "Someone loses; someone wins. That's the way it is. You did okay."

I was being smothered with sympathy. I had been shit and everyone had seen it. Everyone, including Melanie and Keiko. I wondered if I would fight here again.

I showered and then got dressed in the changing room. I swapped awkward banter with Dave the Masher who kept his stupid smirk on his face the whole time. I felt he was smirking at me, which he undoubtedly was. Still, I was hardly in any position to do anything about it.

I walked to the car with Melanie and Keiko. We barely said a word. We hadn't gone to the Fucking Room while another fight took place. I was too dejected. Was Melanie disappointed in me?

I felt she was. I felt she wanted me to beat the cocky arrogant bastard into the dust, to *mash him up* in front of her eyes. She wanted to walk off with me arm in arm, her champion and guardian, through the crowd to the changing room, and then to pleasure me in the Fucking Room, satisfying her intense sexual desires — and mine, too.

Instead, I had been humiliated by a better man. If anything, she should have gone off with him. He was younger, leaner, meaner, and *well fit*. Yes, if this had been a K1 match, she would have been hanging outside the changing room door for him, awaiting entry so she could service him and satisfy her lust. Instead, she was dragging home the beaten dog with his tail between his legs. The victor was elsewhere.

After dropping off Melanie and Keiko, I went straight home. My condoms remained in my wallet. They weren't needed. I slept alone that night and with little sleep. I was worried about what Mitch said to me before I left the Hope and Anchor.

He took me one side and said. "You did well tonight, son, but fucking 'ell, are you sure you want to carry on doing this? You're going to have one hell of a shiner tomorrow morning."

"Yes, I'm sure. Why do you ask?"

"'Cause you are losing more than you are winning and you are losing quickly. I'm a little concerned."

"Don't worry about me," I said. "I can handle myself... and I am improving."

Mitch said nothing, but I felt sure Mitch he would not to let me fight again. My fights are over too quickly. He's not getting value for money. I was convinced my life as a pugilist was over.

Fights took place at the Hope and Anchor on the first Sunday of each month. I thought my last fight had been just that; my last fight. If I was to ever go there again, it would be as a part of the audience. I was sure Mitch would never let me fight there again.

I told Melanie my fears and she was delighted. She explained as much as she enjoyed watching me fight, she hated seeing me get hurt and she was happy I was not going to fight again.

However, I was utterly despondent. I wanted one more fight, one more go. If not to win, then at least to lose with some credibility, to give as good as I got, and to give a good account of myself. I wanted my early retirement from fighting to be with some honour, at least.

"You want one more fight?" said Keiko.

It was Saturday morning and we sat around the dinner table in our dressing gowns. I nursed a cup of coffee in my hands. It was a fresh summer's day and the windows were open. It was too early for traffic and the birds sang outside without competition. Normally it would have felt great to be alive, especially as I was sharing the day with two such beautiful women. However, that was not how I felt.

"Yes," I said. "I want another fight."

"Why?" said Melanie, putting down her toast and gazing at me with genuine concern.

I looked up at the ceiling, shrugged my shoulders, and said nothing. The fight had been three weeks ago but the humiliation of my defeat would not go away.

"Are you still brooding about the last fight?" said Keiko.

"I want one more try," I said simply, refusing to be drawn into explaining myself.

"This is ridiculous," said Melanie, getting angry. "You will get yourself hurt again, only this time it might be worse. Have you gone mad or something?"

"Melanie," I said, trying to sound reasonable, but barely able to hide my impatience with her. "It is not ridiculous. It is a sport and a sport only. It is a damn sight less dangerous than sky diving, bungee jumping, or even fucking cricket." The girls looked at me questioningly. "When a cricket ball is hit by a cricket bat," I explained, "the cricket ball becomes a lethal weapon, a missile. You get hit in the head by one of those and you are finished. The world of illegal fighting is safer than cricket, believe me."

"Oh, how fucking stupid do you have to be," snapped Melanie impatiently, "to compare cricket to fighting? Christ, what next. You'll be comparing fighting to bowls, next."

"Oh shut up!" I snapped. "You're the one being fucking stupid!"

She stood up, knocking the chair backwards onto the floor, and stormed into her bedroom, slamming the door behind her.

The birds continued to sing outside.

"Melanie's upset," said Keiko.

"You think?"

"She cares for you. That's why she's upset."

"She has a funny way of showing it."

"Love does express itself in funny ways," said Keiko.

"Yes, I guess it does," I said.

A couple of minutes later, Melanie came storming out of her room, marched across the living room to the front door, opened it, marched out, and then slammed the door behind her. We heard her steps clumping down the staircase.

I showered, dressed, and then went back into the living room. Keiko was in the kitchen, washing the dishes. I joined her. She looked up and smiled at me.

"Another cup of coffee?" she said.

"No thanks."

I started wiping the dishes.

"Do you still want to fight again?" asked Keiko. I nodded. I wasn't in the mood for words today. "It might not be easy," she said.

"Why not?"

"After your last fight, Mitch might not think you are up to it."

"I am up to it," I said, without any confidence whatsoever.

"I know," she said. "But will Mitch see it like that?"

"Can you at least ask him?"

"I will. In the meantime, you should try and make it up with Melanie."

Melanie came back forty minutes later. Her face had lost the red glow of anger. She seemed to have calmed down.

"I'm sorry," I said. "I shouldn't have told you to shut up. It was rude and inconsiderate of me."

She sat down on the sofa and kissed me on the cheek.

"What about the fight?" she asked. "Is it going ahead?"

"I've asked Keiko to get Mitch to set one up. Look, if you don't want me to fight, just say the word and I won't, but hear me out first. I have to go into the ring to fight for my self-confidence."

"So it is only about your ego," she said, without malice.

"No, I mean, to a certain extent, I suppose it is; but it is more than that. I have to prove to myself I can make a good showing, that I can do myself proud. My last fight was a bloody disgrace, a complete farce. I was humiliated by that fucking gypsy."

"Gypsies are good fighters, Freddie. It is no disgrace to lose to one of them," said Melanie, kindly.

"No; but to lose so ignominiously is a disgrace. I want another chance."

She leant over and kissed me on the cheek.

"You only have to prove this to yourself. You have already done it for me."

"I want you to be there to give me encouragement."

We embraced one another.

"Of course I'll be there," she said. "You can count on that."

Keiko came in from her room with her portable phone still in her hand.

"Guess what," she said, as we both looked up at her. "I've spoken to Mitch and the fight is on, if you are still interested, that is?"

"I'm interested," I said. "When's the fight?"

"Next Sunday."

"Christ. That doesn't leave me much time for training. I better get started. Who am I fighting?"

"Dave 'The Masher' McNealy."

The gypsy! Oh Christ! Not him again. Outside, the birdsong had long been drowned out by the traffic.

Chapter 16

Once in the Face Is All It Takes

I trained like fuck. I explained to Terry the circumstances and he suggested I intensify my training and concentrate on my punching. He sparred relentlessly with me, passing on his knowledge of fighting, showing me how to duck and weave, how to parry blows, and to deliver them.

I shadow boxed. I punched the heavy bag. Every morning I got up at half past five and ran five miles. Then I skipped with the jump rope for ten minutes.

I showered and had breakfast. I stuck to a strict diet as suggested by Terry and drank only water. By the following Friday, I felt I could take on the whole world.

As usual, I drove into the car park with Melanie and Keiko and then we walked from there to the Hope and Anchor.

"How are you feeling?" asked Melanie, as we stood before the door. It was early evening, still light, and there was little traffic in the street. The three of us were alone outside the pub, from which there was little sign of the activity that would be taking place in the cellar below.

"Nervous," I replied truthfully, "but confident."

She kissed me on the lips and said, "You will do splendidly. I'm sure."

Keiko kissed me on the cheek.

"Melanie is right. Go and slay him and bring Melanie his head."

We laughed and then made our move. Once inside, I nodded at the bar tender and with a jerk of his head, indicated we were to follow him down into the cellar, which we did. Once we were through the door into the cellar, the same sight greeted us as before. The musty air was full of cigarette smoke and people were milling around in small groups talking to each other. A few turned around to look at us and then turned away. A few eyes lingered a little longer on Melanie and Keiko, which I quite understood.

They both were dressed well. Melanie wore a short skirt and a tight blouse. I was there to fight for her, to impress her, and she knew it. In her own way, she was giving me encouragement, even spurring me on. She had originally been angry at me for wanting to fight again, but now, I was sure, she was looking forward to it with eager expectation. Oh God! I so much wanted to win this... for Melanie.

"'Ow are you, son?" said a voice to the left of me. Mitch thrust his fat hand into mine. We shook. "Ready for the fight?"

"Ready and confident," I said.

"I'm sure you'll do well," he said. "You know you're fighting Dave 'The Masher' tonight, don't you. You're first on the bill. We'll be kicking off dead on seven, which gives you ten minutes to get ready. Any questions?"

I shook my head.

"No, I'm fine," I said.

"Are you ladies, okay?" asked Mitch. They nodded and smiled. He looked back at me. "Great, well, you know where the changing room is. I'll give you a shout when it's time to come out."

As he walked away, I said, "I'm going to get changed. I'll see you when the fight is on."

Melanie grabbed hold of my head with her hands and gave me a full kiss on the lips, such as I never had before.

"You are going to be magnificent," she said.

"Thank you. I won't let you down."

I went to the changing room and Dave "The Masher" McNealy was there in person.

"How you doing, me ol' bruv?" he said, flashing me that arrogant and cocky smile of his.

"Fine," I replied, and then added with a jocularity I did not feel. "I'm looking forward to winning the fight."

"Jesus, are you really? Have you changed tactics since last time," he said, with a huge grin. "I fucking hope so. Do you know, I've got a terrible, terrible feeling you will be one of the lucky ones tonight."

"Really," I said, surprised.

"Really," he said, not breaking his grin even to speak.
"You'll be one of the lucky ones to go home early."
He cackled a dry laugh and I smiled.
"Maybe," I replied, lamely, "But as the victor."
"Ha ha, we'll see, we'll see."
We both got dressed into our trunks and then Mitch came in.
"You're both on," he said.
We walked out of the door to the applause of the crowd. The only
light was above the arena. We walked up to the gate in the fence and
went through. Melanie and Keiko were there, looking at me through the
wire fence. I smiled at them and they smiled back.
Mitch was in there and his voice boomed out.
"Ladies and gen'lemen. The first round tonight is between Dave
'The Masher' McNealy..." There was a huge round of applause from
everyone, apart from Melanie and Keiko, who held a stoic silence. "...
and Freddie 'The Gentleman' deFord."
Freddie *"The Gentleman"* deFord? There was another round of applause, but this time a little more restrained. Melanie and Keiko, however, clapped loudly.
"You know the rules," said Mitch. "There are no fucking rules except you do as I tell you. Okay?" We both nodded. "Let the fight start."
Mitch pulled back. Dave "The Masher" McNealy and I squared up
to one another and put up our fists. His stupid grin was still spread
across his face and I wanted desperately to wipe it off. Dave stepped
forward and threw one hell of a punch, but I was expecting that, so I
darted to one side and threw him a punch that landed directly into his
face, knocking him back.
Terry's words from training came back to me. *Follow it up. Once you
get an advantage, follow it through and to the finish. It may never happen
again.*
I rapidly followed it through with another punch before he could
regain his balance... and then another... and then another. He stumbled
and I threw the biggest uppercut I had ever thrown in my whole life.
He flew through the air and landed with a thud on his back. The
arrogant grin was well and truly wiped off his face. There was a dazed
look in his eyes. There was a cry of disbelief from the audience. Someone in the back shouted out.

"Go on, my son! Finish 'im off!"

The thought soared through my head. *My God, this is it. I can win this.* I was knocked out of my reverie by the sight of Melanie standing there, silently but expectantly.

"Go on Freddie!" her eyes seemed to say. "Finish him!" There was a glow to her. It may have been my imagination, but I felt that she had an over-whelming desire, a desperation even, to see me do some real physical violence. She wanted me to beat him up right in front of her.

"Go on, Freddie," I heard Keiko shouting, her face a broad smile, her eyes also wide. "Finish him." As she shouted this, she discreetly jerked her head in Melanie's direction. Keiko understood. Beat this piece of shit up *for Melanie* and it will give her a sexual high.

Dave stirred on the ground. I jumped up and landed on top of him, winding him, his head bobbed up in surprise.

I looked up at Melanie as if to say, "Are you ready for this." Her mouth was agape and her eyes wide.

I raised my fist and started pummelling Dave's face. Again and again. He was helpless. My legs held his arms down on the ground. His head was open to unprotected punches from me. And so I punched and punched and punched. First his lips broke and bled; then his nose broke and bled profusely; then I closed up one eye. Wack! Wack! Wack! The sound of skin and tissue and bone breaking make a sickening squelching and cracking sound.

I was aghast by the sight below me, but I would have carried on just to please Melanie. I would have killed him to delight her. I would have taken up Keiko's suggestion and cut of his head and offered it to her.

A voice boomed in my ear, "Stop the fight, for fuck's sake!" A pair of giant hands lifted me under my arms and pulled me off. "You've won, for fuck's sake." Mitch lifted my right arm above me. "Ladies and gen'lemen. The winner. Freddie 'The Gen'lemen' deFord."

The auditorium erupted into applause. Melanie was grasping her hands and cheering and dancing on the spot. Keiko was smiling broadly and clapping enthusiastically. I raised my fist and smiled at the crowd. The gate opened and friends of Dave "The Masher" McNealy rushed in and bent over him. He was conscious but dazed.

I walked over and said to a young man with a trilby on his head.

"Is he okay?"

"He'll be fine. Don't worry. You did well."

I smiled down at the prostrate body.

"So did he. So did he." For the first time, I felt a genuine affection for the man, sparked, I expect, by a feeling of kindred spirit.

I walked through the gate to more cheers and was patted on the back by well wishers. Melanie threw her arms around my neck and I threw my arms around her waist, lifted her up, and swung her around twice.

"You were wonderful," she said, fighting back the tears. "Truly, truly wonderful."

"I did it for you," I said into her ear.

"I know," she said, kissing me. "I know."

"Come on," I said. "I gotta get dressed."

I took her into the Fucking Room. I slipped off my trunks and Melanie was out of her dress and underwear in seconds. She sank to her knees, took my prick into her mouth, and started sucking greedily, her tongue teasing and tormenting my twitching cock, and her head going back and forth, back and forth. My prick stiffened and became erect. She withdrew and stood up.

"Freddie, sit on the sofa, please," said Melanie.

I went over to the sofa against the two way mirror. I saw the second fight was about to take place. I sat on the sofa with my back to the mirror and the ensuing fight. Melanie came over to me and stroked my cock, making sure it would stay hard. She then grabbed hold of my shoulders and lifted herself on to me, her legs sliding past me, her cunt lowering itself onto my prick. I supported her weight by holding on to her bottom. She started bobbing up and down, her small but perfectly formed breasts slapping me rather deliciously in the face.

I could hear the fight beginning to take place behind me. I knew Melanie's eyes would be focused intently on the fight, relishing every minute of it, taking it all in, wanting more.

Her bobbing became frantic.

"Oh God! Oh God! Oh God!" she cried. She arched her back, her face to the ceiling, and let out an orgasmic shriek I thought would shatter the two way mirror behind us. That would have given the punters a sight, that's for sure.

At that moment, the door burst open, and a man in his late fifties burst into the room. I recognised him. He had been in the audience, but I had given him little thought.

"Ya piece of shite!" he yelled, his fists were clenched and his face, directed at me, was contorted into a mask of rage and hate.

Melanie let out another shriek, this time one of fear. She slid off me and dashed over into the corner of the room, one arm over her breasts and her other hand covering her pussy. Her eyes betrayed her horror and fear.

"Do y'know what ya did to ma son, ya fucking cunt!"

He strode over to me just as I ejaculated. Spunk flew out of my excited prick in an arc, hitting him directly in the face. He stopped in his tracks. His face was covered by a blob of semen. Time froze. Only the fight behind us carried on noiselessly, as if in a silent movie. No one moved. Spunk slowly dripped down his nose and dropped off, like a dew drop, onto the floor. He took out a handkerchief and wiped his face clean.

"Jesus," he said. "Oh fuck!"

With a look of absolute disgust on his face, he turned around and walked out, leaving Melanie and me looking at his retreating back. After he had gone, we let out a sigh of relief.

"I can't believe I saw that," said Melanie, goggle eyed and stifling a laugh. "What the fuck did he want, anyway?"

"I think that may be the father of Dave 'The Masher' fucking McNealy."

"Let's get out of here. He may come back."

Melanie hurriedly dressed and I put my trunks back on. We ignored the mute drama that was taking place behind us through the two-way mirror. I walked up to the door and into the changing room. Dave was there. A doctor was examining his face. His eyes were swollen and his nose busted. His father was there, but did not make eye contact. He obviously had not told anyone what had happened and was not about to. He did not want to become a laughing stock. Without bothering about a shower, I rapidly changed and then slinked out. Mitch met me. Melanie stood by his side.

"You did well, my son. I didn't think you 'ad it in you to win, but fucking hell, you sorted 'im out, all right. Here you are. One hundred and fifty prize money." He handed it to me in twenty pound notes.

I was taken aback. I really hadn't thought about getting a prize. I was just interested in winning. The prize was being fucked by Melanie directly after the fight. That was why I did it. For that reason and that reason alone.

"Thank you," I said, and took the money.

"You up for a fight next month?" he asked. I nodded. "Good. I'll give you a call."

He turned away and Keiko came up to me.

"You were terrific," she said, "Absolutely fantastic."

"We have to go," said Melanie, still freaked out about Dave "The Masher" McNealy's father. She had a point. So was I.

That night, Melanie lay in my arms, her head on my chest. We had made love again. She told me how magnificent she thought I had been in the cage. The one thing neither of us mentioned was the spunk hitting Dave's father in the face, and yet it hung in the air like a bad smell, refusing to go away. To be frank, I knew perfectly well something like that would never go away. I mean, how many times do you accidentally cum in a strangers face? Not often, I should imagine. As a defensive measure, it beat any technique Terry had taught me.

It seemed to me Melanie loved my display of violence for her benefit. We had sex every night. She hung on to my arm the whole time and beamed at me whenever her eye caught mine. Everything had worked out fine. I had overcome the shame of my first fight. I could enter this world of illegal fighting with confidence, keep on impressing Melanie, and win fight after fight after fight. Apart from my intensive training, which I kept up, I was sure it was my yearning—my sexual yearning, after all—that had bought me victory. She had made me what I was. With her by my side, I was unbeatable. And on the following month, I was determined to show her again. Doubts, however, began to hover on the horizon.

The truth was I was never *that* good at fighting and to have beaten Dave "The Masher" McNealy seemed too good to be true. So it turned out. Dave the Masher McNealy, despite the swagger, the bluster, and the gypsy blarney, was just that: Bluster, swagger, and gypsy blarney.

There was no substance to him. Put bluntly, he was no good at fighting.

I didn't realise this until some time later when Mark told me. By that time, I realised I was better than McNealy, but that was all.

Slowly, my life started to unravel.

Chapter 17

A Street Fracas

Melanie and I were getting along like a house on fire. Things couldn't have been better. I had the feeling she looked at me with new eyes. I was no longer just a journalist—even as an editor—but a man who could step inside a cage and show his worth; show that, if necessary, he had what it took to defend her and keep her safe from harm. I was her champion... her guardian. I was there for her. While I was there to protect her, she was safe.

This, as it turned out, would be put to the test.

One evening, after I had taken Melanie out to the theatre to see a play, we went to the West End for a meal, and then afterwards we went on to a pub called The Moorcock. It was a familiar watering hole near my office. I went there often with members of my staff. It was an old fashioned pub with prints on the wall of writers from a bygone era: Chesterton, Wilde, Conan Doyle, and Rider Haggard, to name but a few. It was never crowded. I knew the proprietor and was on speaking terms with many of the regulars. It was a home away from home and I always felt relaxed and at ease there.

However, I was not relaxed today.

We stood at the bar with our drinks. Directly behind me, there was a group of young men. They were rowdy and their language coarse.

"Come on you cunt, get your fucking round in," was one particular example.

I could tell they made Melanie feel ill at ease. She kept looking apprehensively over my shoulder.

I looked her in the eye and said, "Shall we move on?"

"Yes, let's," she replied, looking relieved we would soon be gone.

To tell the truth, I was feeling a little nervous myself and began to inwardly curse the bar staff for not taking action against these drunken yobs. This wasn't a rough house, after all, but a respectable pub. Any other time, Jack, the owner, would have walked over and ordered them to leave. I had seen him do it several times before.

"Okay," I replied to Melanie. "Let's drink up and go."

At which point, one of the guys jostled me, making me spill my beer. I swung round.

"'Scuse me," I said. "Do you mind who you're jostling. You spilt my beer."

They were a group of six young men in their late teens or early twenties. They were casually but smartly dressed, which surprised me. I was half expecting a bunch of tattooed hoodies. They went quiet.

"'Ere, Dave, you spilt his beer," said one of them. "Apologise to the man."

"Sorry, bruv," said the offender, but with a cheeky smirk on his face. "Won't 'appen again."

"Okay," I said, and then turned back to Melanie. I downed my Becks and said, "You ready?"

Behind me, I heard a wolf whistle and then, "Nice bird. What's she like?"

I turned round to them.

"Sorry?" I said, emphatically. "What's she *like*."

"I'm just saying," said the one who appeared to be the ring leader, "you got a nice bird." I gazed at him silently. "It's a compliment. Don't get your back up, for fuck's sake."

"She happens to be my girlfriend and I would appreciate it if you didn't use foul language in front of her."

"Okay, bruv. I'm sorry."

I turned back to Melanie. I began to think the one good thing about training for a cage fight is that it boosts one's self-confidence when it came to confrontational situations, like the one I was in now. We both put down our glasses and began to walk out. As we walked towards the door, a comment followed us out.

"'Ave a good time tonight," said a voice followed by a roar of laughter, and then, "Fuck 'er brains out and then give 'er a kiss from me," followed by more raucous laughter.

I stopped dead in my tracks and steeled myself.

"Come on, Freddie, "said Melanie, taking hold of my arm and giving it a tug. "Let's go. Ignore them. They're just a bunch of idiots."

That they were just a bunch of idiots was not the point. They had insulted me and, more to the point, they had insulted Melanie. My honour had been wounded. I could not let this go. I had fought against McNealy. I had fought against Mark. These were professional underground fighters. What the fuck did I have to fear from these terminal acne cases? I was not going to lie down and let them walk over me, as I would have done normally. I was now a different person. I was a professional fighter. I was a man.

And if this would impress Melanie—all the better.

"Wait here," I said to Melanie. I turned round and walked up to the group of boys in the bar. I tore into them.

"Who do you think you are talking to me and my girlfriend like that? Haven't you pigs got any manners? I swear to God I am *that* close," and I held my hand up and indicated roughly an inch between my thumb and forefinger," to giving you all a good hiding! If you say just one more word, *one more word*, God knows I won't be answerable for my actions! Have you got that?!"

The Moorcock lapsed into silence. The customers and bar staff stared silently in our direction. The gaze of the youths was fixed to the floor. I glared at each and every one of them.

After a moments' silence, I said, "I am going and I don't *ever* want to see any of you lot in here again."

I spun round on my heels and marched back to Melanie, who was standing by the door and looking surprised by my uncharacteristic action. I thought, but couldn't swear, I detected a hint of admiration in her look.

"Come on," I said to her. "Let's go."

We linked arms and marched out the door. God, I felt good. Like most people, I don't usually stand up to roughs like that. I just roll over and hope they don't notice me any more than they have already.

Not this time! I had stood up to them. I had told them where to get off. I had come *that* close to telling them to fuck off. I had done all of this in front of Melanie. I was walking on air. In the bracing chill night of London Town, I felt like a man. At that moment, a commotion erupted behind us.

We turned round. The gang of youths had run out and the leader of the gang, a gangly skinny boy with dark curly hair, glowered at me.

"Who the *fuck* are *you* to talk to *me* like that?" he snarled.

I could feel Melanie's grip on my arm tighten. I unhooked her arm and told her to stay where she was. I then approached the youth. My confidence began to trickle away. The situation was turning uglier by the second and was spinning out of my control. I tried my best to maintain an air of bravado, although panic was beginning to bubble to the surface.

"If I were you," I said, attempting to suppress a quiver in my voice, "I would turn around and walk away with all your friends."

His friends began to spread out, surrounding us, like Indians in a John Ford movie. I felt like General Custer at Little Big Horn. The cool air had turned decidedly chillier. The milling crowd, sensing trouble, was moving away and then standing on the edge of the presumed safety zone, gawping, waiting to see what would happen.

In a funny way, I felt I was behind the chicken wire again. I steeled myself. He stood his ground and glared at me. So this piece of shit wanted a fight. I decided to take the fight to him.

"Okay," I said. "If that is how you want it." I slipped off my jacket and handed it to Melanie. Just as Melanie was about to take it, she let out a shriek and then shouted.

"Get your hands of me, you pervert!" Melanie glared at one of the youths. The youth grinned back at her lasciviously. I was incensed. He had obviously goosed her.

"You bastard!" I shouted and, dropping my jacket on the ground, rushed towards him. I lifted my fist to strike. As I did so, the gang leader leapt at me and started raining down blows on my head. The other one joined in. I stepped back, trying to dodge the blows of both men, and as I did so, lost my footing and fell to the ground. They started kicking me. I covered my head with my arms, so they aimed their kicks at my body. Christ almighty, I was hurting.

As I had my arms around my head, protecting it, I could see nothing.

All I could hear was Melanie screaming, "Leave him alone! Please, leave him alone!"

At the moment, there was a flurry of activity above me. The kicks and the blows had stopped. I removed my arms from my head, opened my eyes, and five feet away from me lay the youth who had goosed Melanie. He lay on his back with blood streaming from his nose. I looked up at Melanie and followed her line of vision. She was looking at a fight between two men. The two fighters were the lanky gang leader... and Eddie Monahan.

Eddie! Fuck! Where had *he* come from?

The youth was fighting a defensive battle. With every retreating step backwards, Eddie took one forwards. Both eyed each other keenly. Melanie, through red, tearful eyes, watched them both.

Eddie suddenly lashed out with his left, striking his opponent in the eye, and then followed it up with a right. The youth collapsed onto the ground. Some of the crowd, the size of which was increasing by the second, even applauded. Eddie turned on the rest of the gang, who had become incredibly sheepish, and roared at them through his rough beard, which, incidentally, was new.

"Come on, then. Bring on the next one. One at a time or all at once, I don't give a fuck." He strutted around, glaring at each of the gang in turn, who, without exception, averted his gaze and backed away from him. "Right, pick up your friends, dust them off and clear off out of here." He came over and lent me his hand. I took it and he lifted me off the ground. I felt I was being hoisted by a crane. "You okay, Dave?"

"The name's Freddie, but yeah, I'm fine. Thanks for your help."

"You were very brave." We both turned to the direction of the voice. It was Melanie. Although her eyes were still red and puffy, they had a glow about them as she gazed at Eddie. She then turned to me.

"You were very brave, as well." She handed me my jacket, which I brushed off and slipped on, and then she kissed me on the cheek. She then kissed Eddie on his cheek. "You guys were both magnificent."

"Come on, you two," said Eddie "Let's scarper before the police arrive. We can have a celebration drink. I quite enjoyed that."

So with Melanie in the middle, like Dorothy, the Lion, and the Tin Man, (or was I the Scarecrow?) in The Wizard of Oz, we all linked up arms and marched through the parting crowd to a little drinking club Eddie knew. In the distance, I heard the sound of a siren. I wondered if this was the police arriving late on the scene.

The drinking club was behind an obscure doorway hidden in a side street of Soho. It was the sort of door that you pass by without giving it a second thought, even though it has a small canopy over the door and a name plate on one side, the name of which I didn't get. Inside was a long bar with a smattering of customers. Small portraits of fighters hung from the walls ranging from Victorian bare-knuckle fighters through to twentieth century boxers such as Henry Cooper and Mike Tyson. This was a fighters' tavern. How appropriate. Behind the bar, there was a large man with a shock of white hair and rolled up sleeves showing massive arms and a collection of tattoos.

"'Ello, Eddie. Watcha goina 'ave?" he asked.

"The usual for me and whatever these two want."

We waited for our drinks and then retired to a table in a dark corner.

"That was some scrap you were in," said Eddie. "What was that all about?" We told him. "Yeah, well, it looks like they picked the wrong person to mess around with. You did well, my son."

"Yeah, but you saved the day. Without you, I would have got pasted," I said, with all honesty.

"Doesn't matter," he said. "The important thing is that you stood your ground and didn't back down."

Then we changed the subject and moved on. Eddie had an up and coming fight next month and he talked about that. In all truthfulness, my mind was far away from the on-going conversation.

All I could think about was my street fight: How I stood up to them in the bar; how I steeled myself for a fight in the street; and how it all went disastrously wrong. I had readied myself for the fight, eager to put my training to the test, willing to defend my woman, and ended up with my woman getting goosed and in a flood of tears and myself on the ground getting a good kicking. Thank God for Eddie. *Fucking Eddie, eh.* He had saved my bacon, but I was not in a gracious mood. There are no two ways about it. He had humiliated me.

Not deliberately. That had not been his intention. Indeed, he admired my stance. He had said so and I had no doubt he meant it. But I had embarrassed myself in front of Melanie, the one person whom I wanted to impress and on whose behalf I had acted. Without her there, I would probably have left those yobs to their beer and walked quietly away.

I couldn't believe how everything had gone so completely wrong.

I sat there listening to Eddie ramble on and on. I looked at Melanie gazing at Eddie with open eyed admiration. It had been Eddie that impressed her tonight. Not me. I had let her down. It had been Eddie who donned the shining armour and rode to her rescue and slain the dragon before her eyes. I bet her heart was pumping wildly when he launched into action, scattering those young men aside. I bet she wanted to go to bed with him in gratitude. He had, after all, earned it.

If I was to make my excuses and leave the drinking club now, which I felt like doing, would Melanie come with me? I doubted it. If I left I would simply have left them alone and they would have ended up in bed together. Not only that, if I had left early, they would have assumed that I was suffering from delayed shock or something and would have made me look an even bigger loser than I thought I already was.

It didn't matter how I looked at it, the whole situation looked bad. If only Melanie was not hanging on to his every word with blatant adoration. If only she would take that silly smile off her face, or at least aim it in my direction once in a while. This was turning into the longest evening of my life.

I excused myself to go the toilet. While I washed my hands, I looked at myself in the mirror. I had a black eye. They were beginning to be quite common.

Chapter 18

Suspicion

"Derek wants to see you," said Siobhan as I came in to the office. She gazed at my black eye without comment.

"About what?" I asked.

She shrugged her shoulder as if to say: *I don't know. He doesn't confide in me. I'm only the bleeding secretary.*

I hung up my coat and walked downstairs to Derek's office. Derek Walken is the owner of *London View*. A 1960s throwback and a mass of contradictions: A millionaire socialist. An armchair activist. A sexual revolutionary monogamist. A gay activist heterosexual. He sat behind his desk, casually but expensively dressed, and smoked a cigarette, which, considering he was in his place of work, was illegal.

"Freddie, sit down. How are you?"

"Fine," I replied, sitting down. "Just fine."

He leant back in his chair, took a drag from his cigarette, and said, "The reason I asked *how are you* is that you are sporting a black eye."

"Oh, that," I said. "I got into a bit of an altercation last night."

"Another one."

I looked up in surprise.

"Another one? No. this is the first scrap I've had since school."

"Really," said Derek, raising his eyebrows. "It's just that, and I'm not the only one to notice this, that you do seem to have sported an assortment of bruises recently and this black eye is simply the worst."

"Yes, it's true. I like to spar. Just to keep fit."

"Highly recommendable, but what is it with the bruises? Shouldn't you be wearing protection for the head?"

"Yes. I do. But they only protect the head, not the face. It wouldn't have helped me last night. Is my black eye a problem?"

"No, not really. I was just concerned, but that is some shiner you have there."

"Well, the black eye hasn't got anything to do with my sparring. As I said, I got into a bit of an altercation. Melanie and I were at a bar and ran into some bloody yobs. They made lewd remarks about her and then one of them took a swing at me."

"Did you tell the police?"

"No, no. I didn't need to. I sorted it out myself," I lied.

"So your sparring came in handy, then?"

I smiled.

"Yes. Some good has come out of it."

"Makes up for the bruising, I suppose."

I smiled again.

"Yes."

"It's not a problem, Freddie, but I do wish you would be a little more careful." He blew out a plume of smoke and then stubbed the cigarette out in an ashtray. "I know you are mainly in the office, but what if we have important visitors to the magazine? I might want to introduce them to my editor and how would it look if I introduced them to someone who looks like he's been in a drunken brawl. I know you don't get into brawls, but it looks like you do. It undermines your authority as editor and makes my magazine look bad. We are also going to have the *London View* Theatre Awards next month and you will be making a public appearance. It won't look good if you make a speech to the assembled audience all black and blue, will it?"

"I suppose not."

"So can I take it when you do make your speech, you'll look less like Brad Pitt in *Fight Club* and more like Robert Redford in *All The President's Men*?"

"Don't worry. I'll be presentable when the time comes."

I went back down to my office and sat at my desk. Every one stared at my black eye.

"Quite a shiner, Freddie," said Abdul.

"What did the other one look like?" quipped Siobhan.

"Did Derek just give you that?" said Eric, making everyone laugh.

"I know you all assume that I got my black eye while sparring, but not this time," I explained, trying to hide my impatience with them. I didn't want to get a reputation as a sourpuss, but I was becoming tetchy about my *other* life. "This time I actually got into a street fight."

Everyone's faces suddenly looked concerned.

"Oh dear," said Siobhan. "What happened?"

I told them the full story, omitting Eddie's contribution and putting myself in his place. My resentment against Eddie grew every time I thought about his intervention, and I was thinking about it most of the time. After I explained myself, everyone was sympathetic and then settled down to work. As did I, but my mind was distracted by my dilemma.

I told Derek I was going to make sure that I would be presentable for the *London View* awards. The trouble was I had a fight lined up for the end of the month.

Should I cancel? It was too late to back down. I suppose I could have cancelled the fight, but I didn't want to put Mitch out, and anyway, I wanted to fight, if only for one more time. I found I loved fighting, but only to impress Melanie. Without Melanie there, the whole thing was pointless, unless, of course, there were other girls in the audience.

If the fight went ahead, I might win and come out unscathed. I might lose and come out unscathed. Either way, Derek would be none the wiser. I decided to go ahead with the fight. If I did come out with two black eyes, a thick lip and a face pulsating with bruises... well, I would deal with that when the time came.

Of course, I realised the purpose of the interview wasn't to make sure I was presentable for the awards. It was a warning. A shot across the bow. Derek didn't want to employ an editor who looked like an East End bare-knuckle fighter, which, in essence, I had become. He wanted a smartly dressed presentable editor, like me, before I became involved in the illegal fight game. He wanted the old me back.

I decided I would have one more fight and then I would quit. I would go back to being the old me. I told Melanie about my decision

"I'm going to quit fighting," I told her.

I was at their flat. Keiko was out. I sat on the settee while she sat in her bedroom checking her mail on the computer. The door was wide open and I could make out her back. Sarah Chang was playing a violin concerto by Karl Goldmark on the stereo.

She twisted her head round and said through the open door, "Good. I'm so relieved. I hated seeing you get beaten up, which happened to you even if you won. What brought on this decision?"

"Derek told me he was not too happy employing an editor who is always black and blue."

"And I want to tell you that I am not happy about having a boy-friend who is always black and blue." She got up from her computer, came out the bedroom and sat down on the settee beside me. She put her arms around my shoulders and kissed me on the lips. "I'm so glad. I always worry about you when you fight. I always think that you might get hurt really bad and when you don't, I'm always so relieved."

"I thought you liked to see me fight?" I said.

"I would rather watch some other man fight. You have proved your physical courage to me several times already. You don't need to keep on proving it."

"I thought it turned you on."

"It does," she said, "but I still fuck you, don't I, even when you are not fighting. We can fuck when watching someone else fight. It'll be more fun, then."

The front door opened and Keiko walked in.

"Hi, you two," she said, slipping out of her overcoat and hanging it up on the wall by the door.

"Guess what?" said Melanie.

"What?"

"Freddie's going to give up the fight game."

"Really. You must be disappointed."

"Don't listen to her Freddie. Just because her boyfriend, Mark, is a fighter, she thinks everyone else should have a boyfriend who fights, as well."

"Melanie, you forget that I know you. You're as bad as I am," she replied.

"I'm not quite as bad as you. Freddie's health is more important and I don't want his face to be continuously battered around. I want him to keep his good looks."

"Talking of which, what happened to you?" Keiko was referring to my black eye. "That shiner is quite impressive."

"Freddie got it in a street fight defending me."

"Really? How thrilling. So the other guy looks even worse than you, at least I hope he does."

"Probably; but not because of me. We ran into Eddie and he rushed over to help us."

"And no-one messes around with Eddie," added Melanie. "We were having a drink and these yobs started causing trouble." Melanie recounted the whole story and then added, "Freddie was very brave. He would have sorted them out himself but they caught him off-guard. That is when he got his black eye. Out of no-where, like the cavalry, Eddie appeared and saved the day."

Inwardly I winced. Melanie was protecting me, trying to make me look good in front of Keiko. I wanted desperately to change the conversation, but Keiko was keen to know every detail. I didn't know if I was being paranoid or correctly interpreting things, but I got the impression when Melanie spoke about Eddie's rush to defend us; she was barely able to suppress her admiration for him. Did she admire him more than me because he succeeded where I failed?

God, I wished I could go back in time and make myself ready for that street fight. If I had been ready, would I still have got trounced? Probably. One thing was clear to me now. If ever I found myself in a fight against Eddie, I would lose. Had Melanie realised that?

My phone rang. The ring tone was coming from Melanie's bedroom. I left my phone in my jacket and my jacket was on Melanie's bed. I jumped up and dashed into the bedroom. As soon as I reached the jacket, the phone stopped. Isn't that always the way? I took out the phone from my jacket pocket to see who had rung me. It had been Siobhan from the office.

I was about to call back when I heard a *ping* sound coming from the direction of the computer. *Incoming mail.* I automatically looked at the screen. It was Melanie's inbox. She had incoming mail. A box popped up saying, *You have mail from Eddie.*

I stared at the message on the computer. Could it be? Eddie! No! Say it ain't so! Oh fuck!

While Melanie continued to chat with Keiko, I ambled over to the computer. Amongst a dozen emails, there was only one from Eddie, but under her *My Folders*, there was a separate folder entitled Eddie.

Eddie? It had to be Eddie Monahan. Who else was there? She obviously had so many emails from him that she had set up a folder especially. How many emails had she received from him, I wondered?

"Anything of interest," said Melanie, appearing unexpectedly behind me. There was a defensive tone in her voice, or was I imagining that?

"No, nothing," I said. "I heard the ping of your email and it attracted my attention. Sorry, I didn't mean to pry."

She strode over to the computer, hurriedly clicked on the mouse, and came out of her email section. *She is hiding something,* I thought, and I knew what it was.

I didn't say a word. I didn't know what to say. I was dumbstruck. Keiko was there and her presence inhibited me. I didn't want a full scale row with Melanie in front of Keiko.

"I've just had a call from my office. I have to go," I lied. I kissed both Melanie and Keiko on the cheek, put on my jacket, and said as I opened the door, "I'll give you a call."

I drove home. My mind was racing. What was going on? Melanie and Eddie? It could have been another Eddie. It is not an uncommon name. However, she had behaved suspiciously. She had crept up on me to see what I was doing. Her tone had been defensive, angry even. She hadn't wanted me to see *something.* Of that I was certain. I could tell by the way she dashed over to get rid of the screen page.

Melanie and *Eddie* emailed each other, but how often? Often enough for her to open a separate folder in which to place all her emails. But how many times? Every day? Once a week? Once in a blue moon?

As I left, Melanie's expression betrayed apprehension. She was worried about something and I knew what that something was: She was cheating on me and I had found out.

This chain of thoughts raced through my mind. I had to know. I wanted to turn round and go back and have it out with Melanie. Oh, fuck Keiko. If she hadn't been there, I would have raised the issue on the spot.

Maybe it was nothing? Maybe Melanie was just thanking Eddie for dashing to her assistance the other day in the street? On the other hand, maybe his fight in the street had impressed her and she had wanted to thank him properly—to show her appreciation by fucking him. That would be Melanie's style. Had I not already witnessed Melanie fuck Eddie in front of my own eyes?

That was it: she was his fuck buddy. After a fight, Melanie could fuck any fighter she liked, even Eddie. I didn't mind that. She was a groupie, that was what she did, that was all part of her sexual make up; but to fuck him any other time meant that it was not just a meaningless fuck after a fight, but personal. It was an affair, and that was the crucial difference. The fact that I was certain she was keeping it secret from me confirmed my worst suspicions.

I arrived at my flat and parked in the bay. I felt wretched and lonely. I could feel Melanie slipping away from me. My beautiful, sweet, sadistic, perverse Melanie. Where would I find another soul mate like her again?

Chapter 19

A Knockout

I would not let Melanie slip out of my life. I had to have it out with her. But a week passed and we didn't exchange a word. The night of my fight was coming close. My last fight. It would be unthinkable if Melanie wasn't there.

I rang her.

"How are you?" I asked.

"Fine."

"The fight is on Friday. Are you going to be there?"

"I can't make it. Sorry."

"Never mind."

"I have an article I have to finish for the next edition."

"It's all right. I understand."

"Good luck. I'm sure you'll do fine."

"Thanks."

I put the phone down and a million thoughts ran through my mind about what she had just said.

That Friday, I drove to the East End of London. The arena in the Hope and Anchor was packed with the usual faces.

Some even acknowledged me with a nod and someone whom I didn't know said, "Good luck to yer, Fred."

I looked around for Dave "The Masher" McNealy and his father, but couldn't see them. Thank God. I really didn't want to bump into *them* again. Come to that, I didn't suppose the father wanted to bump into me, considering what happened the last time, unless, of course, he has developed a taste for getting hit in the face with spunk. I never cease to be amazed for what people get a taste. I suppose some, if not most, people would be a little surprised with my particular taste, although I suspect quite a few girls would not be surprised at Melanie's.

"'Ello, son," Mitch said. "Are you ready for the fight? You'll be fighting Gene Branigan. An ugly looking cunt, but a fucking good fighter."

"I'm ready for whatever you throw at me."

Mitch laughed.

"Good for you. Well, you're on first so good luck. If you fought as well as you fought last time, you'll do fucking brill."

I went into the changing room and changed into my fighting trunks. Gene Branigan was there and Mitch was right, he was ugly looking. A big man; fat, but muscular as well. He had a small nose, a small mouth and small piggy eyes, but his head was large and bald and he had two cauliflower ears.

"You all right, bruv," he grunted. "I think I'm fighting you."

"I think you are," I said, my confidence draining away like water down a plughole.

We walked to the arena together. Gene and I walked through the cage door and into the pen with Mitch. My heart was not in the fight. I looked around and saw no girls at all. If Melanie had been there, I would have wanted to please her with my fighting skills. That she may not care if I won or lost lingered in the back of my mind. I wanted to have it out with Melanie, to sort it out once and for all; but I was scared in case I was right and she was in love with another man.

I could see no girls in the audience at all. The desire to fight drained completely out of me.

The lights went down and Mitch announced us with his usual enthusiasm.

"Ladies 'n' Gentleman. We are going to have the first of a series of fights tonight. Starting off the proceedings is a fight between Gene Branigan and Freddie 'The Gen'leman' deFord." There was a cheer as each of our names was announced. "Okay lads. You know the rules. There are no fucking rules except you must obey my orders at all times. Understand?" We both nodded. "Good. Let the fucking fight start."

Mitch stood back and I faced Branigan. He loomed over me like a mountain of lard. If I punched him, my fist would just sink into him. If he punched me, I would be flattened.

He came up to me and I threw a punch in his face, making contact with his jaw. It was like hitting granite. My fist throbbed like fuck. The punch barely seemed to register with him. He pounced forward and threw his whole weight on top of me. I collapsed beneath him. As I lay under the massive bulk of his body, I could hardly breathe. I tried throwing some punches, but they were ineffective. Not only that, as I couldn't breath, I was beginning to panic.

With a swiftness that surprised me for such a big man, he rose up, straddled me, and then started raining down blows around my head. I fended some off, but a few others found their mark. He then held down one of my arms and started pummelling me with his free fist. I felt a fist ram into my eye. I felt another ram into my mouth. Pain surged through my head. I suddenly felt physically sick. Any moment, I thought, I might throw up. I was trapped, panicking, desperate, in pain, and ready to vomit.

The blows kept coming. My single free arm was ineffective against them. I was just about to slap the floor with my free hand in submission when I suddenly felt light-headed. The sound faded, the lights dimmed, and I passed out.

I woke up in the changing room lying on the table with Mitch, Melanie, and Gene Branigan standing around me, with varying degrees of concern on their faces. I wondered where Melanie had come from.

"He's back to the land of the living," said Mitch. "Thank fucking God for that."

"You all right, bruv?" grunted Gene.

I groaned something everyone found indecipherable. It was meant to convey the fact that my body and face ached like mad and I could only see out of one eye.

"Thank God you are all right," said Melanie, sounding like she was on the verge of tears. "Thank God you are giving this life up."

"Is he giving up the fight game?" enquired Mitch, looking at Melanie in surprise.

"Yes, he is," she replied. "And I'm glad. I mean look at him. He's a complete mess. He can't go on like this forever. He's going to look awful after a couple more fights."

The thought went through my mind Melanie sounded as if she was more worried about having an ugly looking boyfriend than about my actual health. But her words did worry me. According to her, I was a complete mess.

Was I? What did I look like?

I made an effort to rise by myself. Mitch and Melanie stepped forward and gently helped me sit up. I swung my legs off the bench and then stood on the floor.

"I'm all right," I mumbled incoherently. "I want a mirror." At first, no-one understood what I had said.

Why was it so difficult to speak?

After several more attempts, Melanie said, "I think he wants to look at himself in a mirror." Mitch jerked his head over to a corner of the room. I turned round and looked at my reflection in a mirror with my one good eye. I could see Melanie's concern. I did look a complete mess. My eye was swollen shut. I had lost a couple of teeth and both lips were swollen like balloons, hence my difficulty in talking. My face was covered in bruises. I don't know how many punches had found their mark, but those that did had been incredibly effective.

How was I going to explain *this* to Derek?

"I look like the Elephant Man," I said, but it came out as something else.

I looked at Melanie with exaggerated surprise, as if to say, "Where did you come from?"

Melanie, picking up my thoughts, said, "I was concerned about you, Freddie. I couldn't stay away. I had to make sure that you were all right."

If I had known she had been there, I would have gone into the fight with a bit more determination. Who knows, I may have even won. I had gone into the fight thinking that no women were watching and as a result, I had been rubbish.

"Freddie," said Mitch. "I've got a doctor coming over to have a look at you. He'll be here in a mo."

Right on cue, the doctor came walking through the door.

He gave everyone a cheery hello and then said, "Who's the patient?"

I mumbled, "Idiot!" But no-one understood me.

He then looked at me and said, "God, you do look a mess." He took off his coat, put his bag on the couch and then opened it. He put on a stethoscope and proceeded to give me a complete examination. Afterwards, he said, "Nothing serious apart from losing a few teeth. Your mouth is swollen so you will have trouble speaking and eating for a few days, but you will soon be as right as rain. I recommend you see a dentist, though."

"Thanks, doc," said Mitch. He handed some money to the doctor, who thanked him and then left. "You, my son, should get yourself cleaned up." I nodded in agreement. Everyone left and I was alone in the changing room. I looked in the mirror again and wondered what Derek would think about my face. These bruises and the swelling would take forever to go down. I did look like shit. I had fought uselessly. I bet Eddie would have fought on—and probably won. Was that going through Melanie's mind as well?

I dressed, feeling wretched.

What should I do about Eddie? I was burning with jealousy over his interference in the fight with those yobs. The fact that without his intervention, I would have been pounded into dust did not make me the slightest bit grateful. It just intensified my jealousy. Worst of all was the thought Melanie might be having an affair with him behind my back. I did not have proof, but I had evidence, however circumstantial it may be. In my mind it was 99% certain and that was enough.

Was Melanie betraying me? I had to find out. As I came out of the dressing room, Melanie had her back to me while she watched another fight taking place.

Driving into work the following day, my mind was divided. I was desperately trying to think of an excuse to explain my battered face. I was also troubled by Melanie's relationship with Eddie Monahan—which I was certain, existed—and what that meant for the two of us. These thoughts consumed me with anxiety.

I arrived at work. As soon as I walked in through the door, the office came to a standstill as everyone turned to stare at me. I felt like shit and looked like it. My face was a map of bruises. My left eye was puffed up. Both my lips were swollen. I looked as if I had just crawled out of a car wreck. I smiled back at everyone as if nothing had happened. They just carried on staring. I knew I should have phoned in sick. As soon as I looked at myself in the mirror this morning, I realised I would have trouble explaining this away. I could not say I got attacked *again*. It would begin to look as if I was a magnet for trouble. I could hardly say I got it sparring. *Some sparring match.*

It was Siobhan, my secretary, who broke the silence.

"What happened to your face?"

"I had a bout last night, at the gym."

"Did you win?" she asked.

I shook my head.

"No."

"That's quite a beating you took," said one of the staff.

"Yes, it was. However, I am fine, despite appearances. Please, don't worry about me." The one consolation was I could speak properly this morning, despite the swollen lips.

Everyone returned to their work, even though I could tell they were not at all convinced by my statement. Who could blame them? It was pretty lame.

About eleven o'clock, Derek Walken rang and asked for me to see him in his office. I walked down the stairs to his floor full of apprehension. Once I got there, his secretary opened the door for me and I walked in.

"Hello, Freddie," said Derek, with a concerned look on his face. "Take a seat." I sat down. "How are you, today?"

"I am fine," I replied.

"You don't look fine."

"I feel fine."

"Freddie. What on earth happened to you?"

"I had a bout. I lost."

"A bout! Who with? Mike Tyson? You look as if you have been knocked down by a bus."

"It's not as bad as it looks, really."

"It looks pretty bad to me. Can you see out of that eye? It is pretty puffed up."

"Yes, believe me, I can function perfectly well. This will not affect my job."

"We have the *London View* awards coming up on Thursday. You are supposed to be there to give a speech and give out some of those awards yourself." I nodded. "Do you seriously think you can give out those awards looking like that?" I said nothing. "I don't think so. Everyone will be so busy looking at your battered face and wondering how it came about they will ignore the actual awards themselves.

"And there are going to be reporters there. What do you think they will be thinking when they see your face? They will be curious. By God, *I'm* curious.

What is *happening* to you Freddie? How did *that* happen to your face? Are you in some sort of trouble?"

"No. Everything is fine. Seriously. As I said, I had a bout without headgear last night and this is the result. I know. Stupid me. I seriously underestimated my opponent."

Derek relaxed back into his chair and took out a cigarette. He offered me one, but I turned it down. He lit it, sucked on it, and then exhaled a trail of smoke into the air. He then leant forward and looked me in the eye.

"Freddie. I've decided to give you some leave. Give you some breathing space. Get yourself sorted out. And then when you come back, you will, hopefully, be refreshed. I know you feel fine now, but a rest really will do you good. I'm bringing in Catherine to temporarily do your job. She will also be doing the award ceremonies."

"I see," I said.

"Why not go on holiday. Chill out. Have a good time. I look forward to seeing you when you come back."

He stood up and extended his arm across his table. I stood up and we shook hands. I felt like we were saying goodbye forever. I was pretty convinced we were.

I went to the Coach & Horses in Pearl Street, an old fashioned bar that hadn't yet been taken over by a conglomerate and had its character ripped out, sat in a corner, and looked out the window as London passed by me while I knocked down one vodka and tonic after another.

What had happened to me?

I had been fired. That much I was certain. Catherine was going to be temporarily editor. If she did a good job, she would get the post permanently. If she didn't, it would go to someone else. However, that was of no concern to me now. *London View* was a part of my past. I had to think what I would do in the future.

Try for another editorial posting? Easier said then done. Editorial jobs are not abundant. The magazine market is not exactly expanding. Maybe freelance. Yes, freelance. I didn't exactly want to go back to that life, but it seemed the only option open to me. I knocked back my vodka and tonic, got another one, and then thought that maybe life as a freelancer may not be so bad after all.

As a freelance, my time is my own, and I could carry on fighting. I had taken to the life of fighting. Melanie, despite protestations, loved watching me fight. I was sure of it. My face could get battered as much as it liked, I had no employer to explain it to. I bet Melanie would love the idea.

Ah, Melanie. My mind went back to the Melanie problem. The Melanie and Eddie problem. Was there something going on there? I had to find out. I got out my mobile. She picked it up after the first ring.

"Melanie. I've lost my job."

"Oh, Freddie. I am so sorry. Why?"

"I want to talk to you now."

"I can't. I am at work. I'll see you tonight. I'll be home by seven. Freddie, I really am sorry. See you tonight."

By seven, I was still at the Coach and Horses pouring out my story to an incredulous Polish barmaid called Anita.

"So that is how your face became the way it is," she said. "Because you fight?"

"Yup. That's it."

"Maybe you're not so good at it, eh."

"Maybe not."

By eight, I was staggering to my car which was parked in a multistorey car park on Brewer Street. I successfully inched my car down the ramps in the car park, managed to put my card into the machine that lifted the barrier to allow me out, and then my foot slipped and I accidentally pressed down hard on the accelerator. I surged into Brewer Street. A pedestrian leaped out of the way of my car. I felt a sickening jolt as I rammed into the side of a delivery van.

The driver of the van jumped out and examined the damage. A crowd gathered to gawp. The pedestrian I nearly knocked over just stood there. He looked as if he was in shock. I sat in the car, my head against the steering wheel, my eyes closed. I couldn't believe this was happening to me. This was such a shit day.

I fell asleep.

I was woken up by someone knocking on the window of my car. I looked up and saw the pissed off van driver looking down at me.

"You drunk, mate?" he shouted. "Is that what it is? You're drunk and you drove your car into the side of my fucking van!"

I pushed open the door and, with effort, got out. I stood before him.

"Sorry," I slurred.

The other driver moved away, muttering to himself angrily. A siren sounded distantly, getting closer by the second. I leant back on the bonnet and sighed. This day had started off badly and was getting progressively worse. The police car pulled up and two policemen got out.

Half an hour later, I was at Marylebone Police Station. I had been charged with driving under the influence of alcohol. A lawyer had been appointed. The lawyer told me the breathalyser test had been positive, that I would have to attend court and I would most certainly get my driving licence revoked for twelve months.

It was one o'clock in the morning before Melanie came and collected me. We climbed into a taxi. She seemed concerned and kept asking if I was all right. I was. I had sobered up, but felt sick to the stomach about the whole day's events. We lapsed into silence. I looked out the window and watched London pass by. It was dark, silent and quiet. Life had drained out of the city. It was almost as if it were sleeping. Only other taxis and stragglers were about.

"Are you having an affair with Eddie?" I said.

Melanie was silent and then said, "Why do you ask?"

"So you are having an affair with Eddie."

"Why do you say that?"

"You are. You would have denied it, otherwise."

"You are behaving strangely. It's getting to the point where I no longer know who you are."

"What are you talking about? I am me. I have not changed."

"You have. When I first met you, you were an interesting journalist who could talk about anything, and now, you've become obsessed with illegal fighting, which you are not well suited to, but which you think you are."

"So, I am delusional."

"Yes. This is not the man that I knew. I want him back, but I know I have lost him for good."

"I thought you liked men who fight. You are a K1 groupie, for God's sake. I thought you fantasised about men who fight. You love to fuck me after I fight. That's your big turn on."

"I don't want to spend my life living my sexual fantasy. I want someone I can talk to without worrying if he is going to be hurt in his next fight. I don't want that life. When I fuck a fighter I don't want to care about him. I just want to fuck him. I want to keep my personal life and my fantasy life separate. You've confused things. You have blurred the lines."

I looked at her in utter confusion.

"So how come you are having an affair with Eddie Monahan? He's more of a fighter than me, or is he just a fuck friend?"

She turned her head and looked at me in surprise.

"Eddie Monahan. You think that I have been having an affair with Eddie Monahan?"

"Yes, of course. You have just admitted it."

She looked at me wide eyed.

"I have not been having an affair with Eddie Monahan." There was a moment's pause. "I have been having an affair with Eddie Wallis."

I couldn't believe it. She was having an affair with another journalist—she not only has a thing for fighters, but journalists as well. The double irony that I introduced my fellow journalist to her had not been lost on me.

I lay in bed that night, alone, and reflected on the day that had passed.

I had lost my job.

I had lost my girlfriend.

I was certain to lose my driving licence.

Chapter 20

Revenge

I woke up at ten thirty with nothing to do. My head throbbed with a hangover from hell. I rolled over in bed wondering what I was going to do today. Eventually, I got up, undressed, and stood under the shower for ten minutes letting the water cascade over me. I thought back to the time when Melanie and I made love beneath the shower, but the memory did not make me feel horny, just sad at the loss of Melanie. The loss of my driving licence was a nuisance; the loss of my job a real body blow; but the loss of Melanie pole-axed me.

Where was I to find a girl like her again? She had single-handedly cured me of *my little problem*. Because of her and the way she was, I could ejaculate like any normal man when making love. But only with her. Or with someone like her. Where would I find someone else like that? I imagined advertising in the lonely hearts page of my magazine I had edited only a day before. *Man. Late 20s. Looking for a girl who is sexually aroused by watching men fight.*

Keiko.

The name came to me in an instant. It was so obvious. She, too, was aroused by watching men fight. Hadn't she, after all, initiated the Fucking Room? Isn't she a Cage Rage groupie? Hadn't we already had sex once and hadn't she given me a spectacular blow job? She had a boyfriend, though. I had fought him once. Unlike Melanie, Keiko liked to date fighters, not just fuck them and leave them. I was pondering on whether to ring Keiko on her mobile—not her home number, Melanie might pick that up—and ask her for a date.

The phone rang.

Maybe the magazine wanted me to come back straight away? Maybe Melanie wanted to apologise and to say she was ditching Eddie. I stepped out of the hot shower, and dripping with water, dashed to the phone. The screen said the number was being withheld.

I picked it up and put it to my ear.

"Hello."

"Hello, bruv. How are you?" It was Mitch.

"I'm fine," I said, a little startled and surprised it was him.

"Good," he said. "'Cause you took one fucking beating the other night."

"Yeah. Tell me about it. I am still black and blue all over."

"Tell you what, my son. You handled yourself fucking well, even if you did lose."

"Thanks."

"How would you like to have another fight in four weeks time?"

"Great. I'm up for it."

"It'll be on the twenty fifth. You'll be fighting Tom Mullin. Get here by seven thirty."

"You can rely on me. I'll be there on time."

"I know I can. See you there."

The phone went dead. Great. Another fight. I wondered if there would be many girls to see me fight. Maybe I could take Keiko. Even if I was no longer Melanie's boyfriend, I could still fuck her afterwards. She could be my groupie. The idea thrilled me. I fantasised about having Keiko as a girlfriend and Melanie as my groupie. My sex life would be fantastic.

I towelled myself down, put on my dressing gown, went to the kitchen and had a cup of coffee. What about the rest of my life? I ought to make enquiries about jobs, but I had a hunch I ought to go into freelance journalism.

Because of cost cutting, freelance was growing in the profession. It is cheaper just to pay for the finished piece and not for a pension plan, bad news days, sickness leave, annual leave, and all the other non-productive days.

Maybe I could write a book. If *London View* were going to get rid of me, they would have to pay me off. I thought about a sum big enough to allow me to take a year off and write that novel I had been intending all my life to write. I could even write a novel loosely based on Melanie and me.

I contemplated calling Melanie. Maybe it is not over. I could cancel my fight, tell Melanie I no longer cared about fighting, that I would give it up completely, and hope, *hope*, she would dump Eddie Wallis, that he was only a port in a storm and the storm was now over, and she would come back to me. However, my mind slowly drifted towards Keiko.

I drank my coffee and washed up the mug. I didn't cook any breakfast. I can never eat when I have a hangover. I went to my study and went on to the Net. I googled Eddie Wallis, journalist. Nothing, apart from a dentist from Green Bay, Wisconsin, who was also called Eddie Wallis. My resentment against Wallis began as soon as Melanie had told me in the taxi last night about their affair. My resentment had slowly grown and was beginning to push everything else out of my mind. The cunt! I really hated him. *Really* hated him.

My phone rang again. I picked it up and the screen said *Samuel.*

"Sam," I said, putting the mobile up to my ear. Sam is the film editor at *London View* and my closest friend on the magazine. We both share a passion for film, and Bunuel in particulary. I had, after all, started my career in *London View* doing his job.

"You know, I probably shouldn't be talking with you," he said.

"You probably shouldn't. I think I am *persona non grata.*"

"Despite that, and to show how I care nothing about my job, why don't we meet up for a drink?"

"Great. When?"

"I finish at four. Four thirty at the The Harpo Club."

"The Harpo Club! Fuck! I'm not a member. Where is it, anyway?"

"Pearl Street. I'm a member. Just say my name. I'll ring ahead and tell the receptionist you are coming."

"The Harpo, eh. Isn't it all media types in there? I knew we were paying you too much."

I got dressed and arrived in Soho about twelve thirty. I intended to go and see a film but arrived at the cinema five minutes after the film started, so I changed my mind and wandered around Soho for a bit, arriving at Pearl Street. I walked along the pavement and found The Harpo Club. I wondered if Sam had told the receptionist I was supposed to be coming. I decided to leave it until a bit later and continued walking.

I ambled around the streets of Soho until I came across a striptease club called the Mardi Gras, which surprised me as this part of Soho was well away from what I would call the sleazy part. There were no other representations of the sex industry here: No other strip clubs, no porno cinemas or book shops, and no walk-ups. It was all restaurants, nice bars and media type offices. I paid fifteen pounds and walked in.

I found myself standing at the bar. The bar area was rectangular with a bar extended along one side. At the far end was a staircase which took you down to the show. I was the only customer there. Twelve semi naked girls, who were lounging around, briefly looked up at me and then, quickly losing interest, looked away. I sat on a stool and bought a beer. A pretty Brazilian girl called Chica sat down beside me and started chatting. It was a hostess bar, as well; but I didn't have to buy an overpriced bottle of champagne, only a normally priced drink. So, as requested, I bought her a glass of red wine and we started chatting. She asked the inevitable question.

"How did you get your face so badly damaged?"

"I got into a fight."

"You must have lost the fight, huh?"

I told her the whole story, the correct story, with Eddie's contribution included. I was fed up with lying about myself.

"So he must be a good fighter, this Eddie."

I nodded. "The best," I said, in all honesty, "although I am a fighter too."

"You?"

"Yes, me." I told her all about my career in underground fighting. After I finished, I had the attention of all the girls in the bar, all of whom stood or sat around me in a circle. Even the doorman was hovering on the edges, listening.

One of the girls, a Romanian, said, "Do you think one day you will fight this Eddie?"

"God! I hope not. No. Definitely not. I just fight in an underground club. Eddie fights professionally in proper events at the Albert Hall and such like. He way outclasses me. I would like to fight Eddie. I would love to fight Eddie. I doubt it will happen though,"

I was being honest here. I did want to fight Eddie. But not Eddie Monahan. I wanted to fight Eddie Wallis. I really did. I wanted to square up to him in a cage, a ring, a street, a car park, a back alley, any fucking where, and just have a one to one with him. I wanted to hurt him. I wanted that *so* much.

My phone rang. I took it out of my jacket pocket. It was Sam. I put it to my ear.

"Hi Sam," I said.

"Where are you?"

"I'm around the corner in a strip club. I'll be there at Harpo's in five minutes." I put my phone back in my pocket, said goodbye to the girls, leaving behind a bottle of champagne for them to finish off, and dashed round the corner to The Harpo Club. He was waiting for me outside.

"Hi Freddie. God, your face looks like shit, doesn't it?"

"Thanks. You look lovely yourself."

We went into The Harpo Club, bought some drinks and then settled down in some armchairs. Very quickly, the conversation came round to how I got my face so badly beaten and I told him everything; I left nothing out. I realised then that before today, and apart from Melanie and Keiko, I had told no-one about my other life. Now that I didn't have to worry about losing my job, having already lost it because of my hobby, I realised I could tell who the hell I liked.

"So what are you going to do now," said Sam, who had listened to the whole thing in obvious bewilderment, "become a professional fighter?"

"I may have left it a bit late for that, but I have no intention of giving it up. I enjoy it too much."

"Why," he said. "Why do you enjoy it? Do you like getting beaten up?"

"No," I said, and from here on, I lied. "I enjoy the thrill of combat; of pitching myself against another man and seeing who comes out on top. It's the greatest buzz imaginable."

What I didn't say was: *I enjoy the thrill of women watching me as I partake in combat: of pitching myself against another man for the pleasure of another woman. It is the greatest turn on imaginable.*

No matter how honest I was, this was a secret I could not share with anyone who did not already understand. I realise my desire to live my sexual fantasy is weird enough, but my actual sexual fantasy itself defies understanding. I do not understand it. I just go with its flow. I do not expect anyone at all to understand it.

We carried on drinking. At one point, I took Sam to the strip club I visited previously and then later, we returned to The Harpo Club. By eleven, I was pretty drunk and was ranting about Eddie Wallis. By midnight, the Harpo decided we had more than enough to drink. Sam got a taxi home and I waited for one myself. One came. I gave the driver my address and then sat back. The driver turned into Brewer Street and then into Frith Street, passing Ronnie Scott's jazz club. My eyes nearly popped out of my head when I saw who was walking by. It was Eddie Wallis. *The fucker!!!*

I angrily tapped on the glass partition and told the driver to stop, which he did. I jumped out, ran along a still busy for midnight Frith Street, and called out to Eddie. He was walking along the road with his head down, oblivious to the rest of the world.

"Eddie, you cunt!" I cried out. He looked around as I approached him. He looked surprised and dazed.

"Freddie, ho...." He started to say, but I never let him finish the sentence. I threw a punch into his stomach that made him double over and then I threw an uppercut that sent him flying along the pavement, knocking over a dustbin and scattering the contents all over the ground. People stood out of the way, not wanting to get involved, but wanting to watch. Despite my rage, I noticed a few women who had stopped to look on. One of them, a gorgeous Chinese girl, had the faintest of smiles and a *look* in her eyes I knew only too well.

That was unfortunate. I may have stopped it there, but now I had an audience, a woman, and I just had to perform.

"What the fuck was that for?" groaned Eddie, as he lay doubled up on the pavement.

"That is for fucking my girlfriend and here's another one, also for fucking my girlfriend."

I picked him up by his lapels, pinned him against the wall of a restaurant, drew back my fist and froze. I wanted to pummel his face with my fist. I pictured it in my imagination. One punch. His head would crack against the wall and blood pour from his nose. Another punch and his eye would swell up and close. A third punch and his lip would split, causing more blood to flow. It would be easy. He was putting up no resistance. He seemed to go into shock straight away. I let go of him and he just stood there looking at me.

I turned away and noticed the Chinese girl. There was a look of disappointment on her face. She would have loved it if I had beaten him senseless. I could tell. I would have done it for her, as well, whoever she is. Afterwards, I could have gone up to her and kissed her and she may well have returned the kiss in full. She would have relished it — I recognise the signs only too well and look out for them — and that is why I came *that* close to doing it. I let go of him and started to walk away.

Everyone was looking at me. I turned a corner. I felt strange. Empowered, energised; but sick. I wanted so much to cause him real physical damage. There was no cause for it... except for the worse of reasons. Revenge... and the desire to please a girl I didn't even know.

Fuck! *I am getting out of control.* I carried on walking through the back streets wondering what I was turning into.

Chapter 21

A Familiar Face in the Crowd

The phone rang. It was Melanie. I answered it.

"You bastard! You little prick! Why did you do that for? I hate you! Hate you! Hate you!" The phone went dead. I guessed she was talking about what I had done to Eddie Wallis. *Oh God!* He must have told her what had happened.

My head throbbed. I went to the kitchen and took an aspirin with a glass of water. What was it a friend told me some time ago: The water does more good than the aspirin? Something about alcohol dehydrating the brain and that is what causes the hangover. So, I drank another glass of water. I then put on my tracksuit and went out for my morning run. Neither the water nor the run did anything for my hangover, but I had a fight in four weeks time. I had to get into shape.

Four weeks later, I was being led to the cage by Mitch. As I walked through the crowd, I recognised a familiar face. Standing by the chicken wire was Keiko. I acknowledged her and she smiled back. In my head I dedicated this fight to Keiko.

The man I fought was called Tom Mullin. He was a tough opponent. He got several punches through my guard and drove me back against the wall. One punch hit me over the eye, cutting it. Blood ran down my face. I would have to finish this quickly before my sight was completely obscured.

I had to strike quickly. I threw myself at him, raining down several hard blows, which he fended off, but he backed away. One of my punches penetrated his defences and struck him hard in the face. It knocked him to the floor. I straddled him and threw one punch at his head after another. The crowd applauded and cheered me on. I couldn't see Keiko but I imagined her relishing my fighting skills. Mullin slapped the floor in submission. I had won.

I stood up. Mitch raised my arm and announced me the winner. I smiled broadly at the crowd and then looked at Keiko. She smiled back.

When I was let out of the enclosure, I walked up to her.

"Hello," I said. "How are you?"

"Fine. You?"

"Had my ups and downs."

"I've just witnessed one of your ups. Congratulations. A good fight. You're covered in blood."

"I know. I got cut above the eye. Did you enjoy it?"

"Yes." She leant forward and kissed me on the lips. "Why don't you take me out for dinner?"

"Okay. I need to get cleaned up first. I'm covered in blood."

"It's stopped bleeding. Can I come into the dressing room with you?"

"Why?"

"I'm all hot and sticky and I need to shower."

"Here?"

"Why not here?"

"Because the next fight is on in ten minutes and there will be fighters in there undressing."

"I asked Mitch if I could take a shower and he said fine. He said he won't let anyone in until I have finished. I won't be long. It might be an idea to stand by the door, just in case."

I went into the changing room to make sure no one else was there and told her to come in.

"Be quick. I'll make sure no one comes in."

Keiko slipped out of her dress, deftly removed her bra, and then slid out of her panties. Her petit and graceful figure stood naked before me. She stepped into the shower and switched on the water. She closed her eyes, lifted up her face, and delighted in the force of the water as it cascaded over her lithe, soft body.

Keiko produced some shampoo and lathered her jet black hair. The surging water carried the shampoo over her shoulders, down her back, in between her buttocks, and down her long, slender legs. Her body glistened as the shampoo clung to her wet skin. As she rubbed the shampoo over her pert but perfectly formed breasts with both hands, she revelled in the sensitivity of her nipples. Sliding her hand down between her legs, her fingers disappeared into the slit between her nether lips, thrusting themselves deep inside, teasing her clitoris. Her face betrayed the fact a wave of pleasure was sweeping over her.

There was no door or shower curtain and the changing room was steaming up. I stood before her entranced. I had never thought of her as exactly a prick teaser; but here she was, teasing my prick to the limit. My prick stood erect and quivering beneath my shorts.

"Do you want to join in?" she suddenly announced.

I didn't reply, but pulled down my shorts and stepped inside. I stood naked before her. The water spayed over us in a continual and steady torrent. She took me in her arms and kissed me on the lips. She then stood back and looked me over.

She looked intently at my body. As the water streamed over me, the blood began to run down my body. Keiko ran the palm of her hand over my chest, smearing the blood over me until my skin began to turn a watery red. She started to smear me with both her hands. She then stepped back and ran her blood stained hands over her own body, smearing my blood over her breasts, her stomach, and then smearing her pussy, easing her fingers into her slit so that some of my blood was smeared there too. Then she ran her fingers over my chest again and ran her hands over her face, smearing the blood over her nose, her cheeks, her chin. She looked at me longingly as she sucked her blood soaked fingers one by one. The water mingled with blood giving her wet skin a red tinge.

"Lick me out," she begged. "I love being licked out. I've heard from Melanie you're rather good at it."

She leaned back against the tiled wall, standing with her legs apart. A jet of hot water sprayed over us as I fell down on to my knees and pressed my face against her shaven pussy. While gripping her hips, I poked my tongue into her moist cunt. My tongue licked her clitoris, played with it, teased it. She tasted so delicious I wanted to eat her—eat her pussy and then the rest of her.

"Oh yes," Keiko purred, throwing her head back and closing her eyes. "That's nice. That is so nice." A long groan escaped her lips.

She ran her fingers over my shoulders and back, gently at first, then more roughly as my tongue continued to tease her. I felt her body shake and her legs quiver as she raced towards an orgasm.

"Oh God, yes," she cried, her grip tight on my hair. "Yes, that's good. That's so good."

Keiko climaxed. Her body shuddered violently and then went limp. I thought for a moment she was going to collapse on top of me. I pulled my face away. I could taste her juices on my tongue.

I stood up. My prick was more erect, bigger than I had ever seen it before. The blood was now all washed away. Her expression was one of exhausted satisfaction. She gazed down at my throbbing prick and a smile flickered across her lips.

"Shall we do something about this lovely creature?" she said, fingering my prick gently. As she touched it, it twitched violently. "God, it's alive," she said, laughing, and then she got down onto her knees, held my balls in one hand, and ran her fingers up and down my prick. It jerked. She watched it intently, a smile spread across her face. I was worried in case I accidentally ejaculated in her face. I could feel myself ready to come.

She then grabbed me by the buttocks and drew my prick into her mouth. Sucking greedily, she teased my twitching erection with her tongue. She then started sliding it in and out of her mouth, her head going back and forth. My prick felt as if it was going to explode. I looked down at her and thought of her at the fight, excited and exhilarated by the male violence unfolding before her, seeing her turned on by it. Oh God, it was wonderful. I fantasised I was a Samurai warrior and Keiko was a geisha girl who had excitedly witnessed me dispatch several of my opponents with my bloodied sword. I felt myself racing towards a climax, a wave of ecstasy ready to crash over me.

She gobbled greedily. I came: violently, swiftly. A gush of hot cum flew into the back of Keiko's mouth, most of it going down her throat and some seeping out the corners of her lips. She continued to suck hungrily, her cheeks drawing in as if she was sucking on a thick milkshake, as if she wanted to suck me dry so that not a drop of cum would be left in my body. When I could produce no more, she pulled off and stood up.

We embraced. The water cascaded down our bodies, cleansing it of our erotic labours. I watched as my cum dripped from the side of her mouth and down her face and neck, down between her breasts, over her flat stomach, in between and down her legs and ankles, eventually swirling down the drain. The last of the blood was gone.

We both stepped out of the shower. There were two fighters standing there open mouthed. They stared at us and we stared at them, no one knowing what to say.

We shared a taxi to go home.

"How's Melanie?" I asked as the taxi sped through the City of London.

"She's fine. She's going out with Eddie Wallis."

"Has she forgiven me?"

"I don't know. I haven't asked her."

"I felt bad about that. It's just that when I saw him standing outside Ronnie Scott's club, I was drunk and I went into a jealous rage."

"What's done is done. Although I wish you hadn't done it."

"Me, too."

"Why don't we go back to your place? I don't want to go back to my flat tonight."

"Okay," I said.

"Do you think the two blokes who saw us fuck in the shower will say anything?" I asked.

Keiko smiled and shrugged her shoulders.

"I should have asked them if they would like to join in. It wouldn't have been the first time."

The taxi dropped us off at my place and we went to bed together. We didn't have sex, but we spent the following day at home.

Melanie moved in with Eddie Wallis. I moved in with Keiko. I continuously wrote and trained and once every month, most months anyway, I would fight. Fighting had become a passion with me. Keiko would watch me and afterwards we would go to the Fucking Room and fuck. Her career took off and her photos were continuously published in magazines and newspapers. She continued to be a groupie.

Two months later, I was officially *let go* from my job. I took to free-lancing and had a number of pieces published in the broadsheets. I was given a tidy little sum by *London View* which I figured would tide me over for the next twelve months if I didn't fritter it away.

One afternoon, Sam phoned.

"How would you like a permanent job," he asked.

"Doing what?"

"Film reviews."

"Are you serious? Who for?" He named the magazine. It was a week-ly periodical. "You're joking. How come they're interested in me?"

"I'm friends with their features editor. He read your piece on Scors-ese and DeNiro in the *Times* and was impressed. He wants to have lunch with you. Are you free on Saturday night?"

"I am now."

"Okay. He will meet you at seven o'clock at a restaurant in Isling-ton. It's called Che's and it's in the high street. Do you know it?"

"Yes."

"Good. Wear a tie. His name is Henry Bennett."

I was over the moon. As soon as Keiko came home, I told her.

"What about your face?" Keiko said.

I looked in the mirror. Fuck! There was a cut above my swollen eye from a recent fight. It made me look awful. I stared at the floor despon-dently. What was I to do?

"Can you put it off until it has healed?" suggested Keiko.

"I can't," I said. "Someone else might jump in before me. This is an opportunity for me to write for a prestigious magazine. I won't get another chance like this."

"If he asks about your eye, maybe you could just tell him the truth."

"Maybe," I replied. "Maybe."

I arrived at Che's at the appropriate time. I wore a suit and a tie. I also sported my cut black eye. This morning, I looked in horror at it in the mirror. The bruising had got worse. It was multi-coloured. It would be impossible to miss.

Keiko suggested make-up, but it was too far gone for that. Anyway, I would have felt, and looked, stupid with make-up on. Even at its most subtle, make-up is obvious to anyone.

I walked into the restaurant. It was dimly lit and there were large pictures of Cuba in the 1960s: a young Castro making a speech before a bank of microphones, Che Guevara smiling through a cloud of cigar smoke, and cheering crowds welcoming in the revolution. All very radical chic. I looked around. In the corner sat a man by himself. He was fat, wore a pin stripped suit and a colourful tie. He looked up and smiled at me. I walked over to him.

"Mr Bennett?" I asked hesitantly.

He got up and extended his hand.

"Call me Henry," he said, "and you must be Freddie." I smiled and we shook hands. "Sit down," he said. "I took the liberty of ordering a bottle of wine. Do you like red?" I nodded. "Good." He poured me a glass and then one for himself. We clinked glasses and then sipped the wine. He offered me the menu. I selected and then the waiter took our orders. The thought of my black eye played on my mind the whole time.

"So you are interested in the post of film reviewer?" said Henry. I nodded. "I've read some of your stuff. It's good. I'm impressed. You write well. You know Ellis Harding, our present reviewer, is retiring at the end of the month." I nodded. "Well the post is vacant. We've got candidates, obviously, but my inclination is to go for you. You have an interesting slant on cinema. You have a wide breadth of knowledge. Also, you know how to write a long piece, and long pieces are what we want in the magazine. So how would you like to write for us?"

"I'd love to," I said and smiled in appreciation.

"Good," he raised his glass, "We'll send you to a few screenings and you can write them up. If we like your reviews, we'll publish them and then we can discuss your future with the magazine."

I happily agreed. I felt I had the job in the bag, although I would have to pull out the stops to ensure the reviews were exactly what they were looking for. I was confident I could do that.

After we discussed my remuneration for the reviews, should they choose to publish them, Henry sat back in his chair, looked at me quizzically, and then smiled.

"May I ask you something?"

"Sure. Go ahead."

"How did you get your black eye?"

This is the moment I had been dreading. I had been running several lies through my mind on my way over here:

I got mugged in the street only last night.

I do sparring and… well, I should have worn some protection, but as you see, I didn't.

My girl friend has a bit of a temper. She's very violent, you know.

My girl friend's lover/ boyfriend/ father came home unexpectedly, found us in bed, and… well, was not best pleased.

Instead, I followed Keiko's advice.

"I got it fighting. Once a month, I fight in a pub basement in the East End of London. It's a hobby."

Once having said it, I wasn't sorry. I was glad. I was fed up with pretence, with lies. Lies had created nothing but trouble for me and eventually lost me my job. It was time to tell the truth and to be honest about what I liked to do.

Henry raised a quizzical eyebrow.

"Really," he said. "How interesting. You know, after the meal, you should let me take you to a club I frequent. It has some people you might like to meet."

It was my turn to raise an eyebrow. *People?* Why would I want to meet anyone *he* might know? Who are these *people* I might like to meet? Are they fighters, fans of fighting, fighters' groupies, other participants in other illegal sports… or what? I didn't like the sound of it. However, I was at a disadvantage. This guy was offering me a *good* job that I needed. The last thing I wanted to do was upset him by turning down his invitation, or even looking sceptical about it. I decided to go with the flow.

"Really," I said, trying to sound genuinely enthusiastic. "It sounds interesting. I would love that."

We didn't return to the subject again. Throughout the meal, we talked about my job: The conditions, the pay, the trial period, and then went on to talk about recent releases in movies and the future of the cinema. It turned out he was a fan of cinema and quite knowledgeable about it. The meal and conversation went on for about two and a half hours.

After we finished the meal and had a cognac, he asked me if I was still interested in going to the club he had mentioned earlier on. I smiled and nodded.

We got a taxi to Soho. When it dropped us off at the club, I recognised it straight away. It was the club Eddie had taken Melanie and me after the street fight. I recognised the small canopy over the door and the name plate on one side. As we went in, I remembered the long bar and the portraits of fighters hanging on the walls. Last time, it had been almost empty. Now, along the bar, there was a line of men perched on stools drinking and talking to one another.

The customers were all middle aged. Some wore suits. Others were casually smart. I don't know why, but they all had an air of illegality about them. One, a tough looking bald headed man, had a scar down his face. I felt I had stepped into a scene from a gangster film.

"What will you have?" asked the barman. I recognised him from last time. He was the large man with a shock of white hair. His sleeves were rolled down and his collection of tattoos was not on show.

"A vodka and tonic."

I got the drinks in. Henry and I stood at the end of the bar. I was curious to see where this was going. I soon found out.

"When you said you were in the illegal fight game," he asked, not bothering to keep his voice down, "Were you being serious?" I nodded. He smiled. "You know, I might have a proposition that may interest you. Hang on. I'll be right back." He went up to the bar, talked to another man whom I couldn't see because he was blocked from view by several other customers, and then came back.

"How would you like to take part in an organised fight at a mansion in Essex?"

"A mansion in Essex?"

"Yes."

"Seriously?"

"Yes."

"You do realise I am on the bottom rung of the bottom league and that is where I am likely to remain. I'm not exactly one of the top names in the game. It is more of a hobby than anything."

"I know. It doesn't matter."

"Okay. Tell me more."

"Come with me." He led me along the bar, stopped, and introduced me to a man in an open necked shirt and a cravat.

"Freddie, this is Damon Nicholls: Damon, Freddie."

We shook hands.

"How do you do?" Damon Nicholls said. "I understand you fight in an illegal fight den once a month." I nodded. "Is it the Hope and Anchor?" I looked surprised and Damon laughed. "How is that old rogue, Mitch?"

"Fine," I said.

"Good. I'll tell you what this is all about. I live in a house in Essex. Big place. Twenty acres. Big trees all around it. You can't see the house from the road. Real private, like. I'm celebrating my fiftieth next month and I'm throwing a party. To keep my guests entertained, I'm going to arrange a series of fights. I'll give you three hundred pound to take part. A grand if you win. Are you interested?"

"Yes," I said, smiling. Three hundred would be nice. Depending on the quality of my opponent, I might even win. That would be another thousand. It is also a party, which means there will most likely be plenty of ladies wearing their party dresses spurring me on. I would be in my element.

"Let's drink to your success in the fight," he said. He ordered a bottle of champagne, poured all three of us a glass, and then toasted my success. Afterwards, he asked me about the Hope and Anchor.

"Tell me," he said. "Do they still have the Fucking Room there?"

Chapter 22

Fighting Naked

We drove along the long tree lined drive. Keiko was at the wheel as I had lost my license several months before. The sound of gravel crunched beneath the wheels of the car. Before us loomed a huge mansion.

"Here we are," I said.

"Impressive, isn't it," said Keiko, as her eyes travelled along the broad front of the house. "I wonder how many bedrooms it has."

"Thinking of staying the night?" I asked.

"Only if I get an offer," she replied cheekily.

"With that dress, you should."

She should, too. It was a long blue dress that was backless, and with a cleavage that plummeted straight down to her waist; but the cleavage was narrow, so that there was only a hint, or a peek, of her breasts. To complete the tease, it was split right up one leg.

In front of the house there were a number of cars parked. Some expensive ones, as well: Rollers, Bentleys, Mercedes. She found a space, pulled in, and brought her Peugeot 106 to a halt. I leant over and kissed Keiko on the lips. She returned the kiss in full. Our lips lingered for a short while and then we separated.

"I'm sure you will fight brilliantly, today," she said, reassuringly.

"With you spurring me on," I said, "I can do nothing less."

We smiled at each other, kissed again, and then got out the car. I was dressed in trousers and t-shirt and carrying a large sports bag. Keiko, clutching her handbag, totted unsteadily on the gravel path, which was unsuited to her high heels. We made our way across the grounds. We got on to the stone pathway that trailed across the expansive lawn and Keiko found a steadier step.

We arrived at the house. Keiko was right. The house was impressive. It was a Regency period pile of grey stones. Countless windows, pitch black because the sun was on the other side, stared like dead eyes over the vast estate, which stretched into the distance. We climbed the stone steps and were greeted by Damon himself. He had on a dinner jacket and was all smiles.

"Welcome, welcome," he said, shaking me by the hand, and then looking at Keiko, said, "Welcome, my dear. Delighted you could come."

He ushered us into a huge hall with a marble floor, statues residing in alcoves, two chandeliers hanging from the ceiling, and a giant staircase sweeping majestically down from the floor above.

"I'll tell you what, my dear. I'll let a servant take you to the party. It's in the garden behind the house. I'll take Freddie where he has to get changed." A servant appeared from nowhere and whisked Keiko away. "Follow me," he said, leading the way up the stairs. "Did you have trouble finding the place?"

"No. We have a sat-nav in the car."

"Marvellous things, aren't they?"

We arrived at the top of the stairs and then turned along a corridor. He stopped abruptly and opened a door.

"This is where you can change. When it is your turn to fight, you will be brought down. Okay?"

"Okay," I said. He smiled, wished me luck, then walked briskly back down the corridor.

I went in through the door and closed it behind me. I found myself in a huge room with plush sofas and armchairs scattered around. Old paintings in gilt frames hung from the wall. The silence was broken only by the loud ticking from a grandfather clock that stood in one corner.

Yet, it wasn't the plush furnishings that initially caught my attention. It was the people sitting around. Sixteen men stripped to the waist sitting patiently on the sofas and armchairs. It reminded me a bit of a doctor's waiting room.

A uniformed butler stood in the centre of the room.

"You must be Freddie deFord," said the butler.

"You must be the butler," I replied, creating a ripple of chuckling amongst the group.

"No flies on you, are there," said the butler, sardonically. He then indicated a door. "You can go through there to change. You need only strip down to your waist." He took out a wallet from his jacket, opened it, and took out six fifty pound notes. "This is your payment for this afternoon. If you should win, you will get a further one thousand pounds."

He handed me the money. I took it and then went through the door indicated. It was a bedroom with a large shower unit and a sink. Scattered around the room were various bags and clothes. It looked like a bedroom at a party, which in a way, it was. I dropped my bag onto the bed, stripped off my t-shirt, and placed it in my bag along with the money. I then went back, shirtless, into the room.

The butler had gone. The room was silent. No-one was making eye contact with anyone else.

Someone finally broke the silence. It was a sinewy man with tattoos covering his body.

"Who is this fucking cunt, anyway? He must be fucking loaded. Look at the size of this fucking place. The fucking paintings alone must be worth a million each."

"*Sir* Damon Nicholls," replied a deep voice, which boomed out of a bald-headed giant with no chin. "He owns a construction company, can't remember which one, and he's made billions."

"Fucking billions is just about right," said the sinewy man with tattoos. "Just look at this fucking place."

The door opened and the butler walked in.

"Mr Stone and Mr Dabrowski." Two of the seated men got up. "Please follow me." We watched them leave. No-one said anything. I stood by the window and looked out over the grounds at the front of the house. I searched out Keiko's car among the many parked on the gravel. I found it. There was something comforting in its familiarity.

Thirty minutes later, one of the fighters, Mr Dabrowski, came back, accompanied by the butler. Mr Stone was nowhere to be seen.

Mr Dabrowski looked dazed.

"They use sticks," he said in a thick Polish accent. Everyone in the room looked silently on.

"Sticks," said the tattooed man. "You mean cudgels. Fucking cudgels."

"Mr deFord and Mr McNealy," said the butler. "Please come this way."

McNealy. The name struck a chord.

Someone, whom I assumed was McNealy, rose up from an armchair which had been facing a window with its back to everyone else. I hadn't even realised someone had been sitting there. When he turned around, recognition struck me in an instant. Dave "The Masher" McNealy.

Oh fuck! I wondered if he recognised me.

"Oh fuck! It's you, you cunt!" he said.

He *had* recognised me. I looked at his face. The arrogant and cocky posturing of the past had been replaced by a mask of pure loathing. He had not forgiven me for the beating I'd given him. I looked at his broken nose. I felt sure it was me who had broken it.

"Dave," I said, with a cockiness I really didn't feel, "I admire your balls, if nothing else, especially after the last time we met." I felt impelled to show a certain bravura.

"You admire my balls, you fucking cunt," he snarled. "Well I'm going to rip your fucking balls out of your fucking scrotum and ram them down your fucking throat, you little gobshite!"

Everyone was staring at us in amazement.

"You two friends?" some wag said.

"Once you two have finished reminiscing," said the butler, impatiently, "Will you both follow me? It is now your turn."

We followed behind the butler. We went along the corridor, down the wide staircase, and along the hallway. We walked in silence but I could sense McNealy's malevolence. He was going to get even, at whatever cost. No quarter was going to be given. I would have to be on my guard.

We arrived outside. There was a large group of people milling around the garden: Men in dinner jackets and ladies in long dresses. On our arrival, everyone looked in our direction. The butler led us through the parting crowd and into a tennis court which was surrounded by ring fencing. The nets had been taken down. There was a young girl standing in the centre of the court.

She was very slim, very pretty, and wore a very short leather dress, which showed off her shapely legs rather nicely. It also showed off her cleavage to rather a nice effect. Smiling at us, she indicated we should stand on either side of her. So we did.

Overhead, the sun shone. A cool breeze swept across the court. I looked through the ring fencing at the faces on the other side. I was reminded of the chicken wire in the Hope and Anchor. I examined our audience.

They were spread along the ring fence silently gazing at us. I felt like a monkey in a zoo. Everyone seemed to be holding a glass of champagne. I saw a waiter walking around filling up empty glasses. There were a number of good looking women. Most were with men, but some stood in groups.

This is what I wanted: An audience of excited women to spur me into action. Without them, I couldn't fight.

I spotted Sir Damon Nicholls standing in the centre with a bunch of dinner jackets — and Keiko. He had obviously taken her under his wing. I was determined to put on a good display for her. I smiled at her and she smiled back.

"Ladies and Gentlemen," shouted the young girl in a rather nice Home Counties accent. "For the second fight today, we have," she looked at a piece of paper in her hand, "Mr deFord and Mr McNealy." There was a round of applause.

She turned to us and said in a much quieter voice, "This is a no-holds barred fight. You will fight until I blow my whistle. When I blow my whistle, you will stop fighting, and then, Mr McNealy, you will re-tire to *that* corner of the court, " she indicated a corner of the court with her finger, and then, looking at me, indicated the opposite corner, "and you, Mr deFord, will retire to that corner. You will both find a cudgel. You will then carry on with the fight, — if you are both still in the game, that is, — using your cudgel as a weapon. Do you have any questions?"

"Yes," said McNealy, "and who might you be?"

"My name is Sophie Nicholls," she said smiling. "I am the referee today."

"Is that your daddy?" I said, indicating Sir Damon Nicholls, stand-ing next to my Keiko.

She nodded her head.

"But enough about me. I want a good dirty fight." She stood back, put a whistle in her mouth, blew, and said, "Let the fight begin."

We squared up to one another. McNealy put up his fists. I put up mine. The audience, anticipating a good fight, stirred. McNealy stepped towards me and threw a couple of punches. The blows whisked past me. I threw a couple of jabs in quick succession which failed to find their mark. I jabbed again.

Taking me by surprise, he grabbed hold of my wrist as I threw a punch, and pulled. I lost my balance and fell flat on my face. I twisted around so I was facing upwards and saw him fall towards me. He landed on my stomach and winded me. He quickly straddled me and rained down blows at my head. One broke through the desperate defence of my arms and landed right in my nose.

Pain surged through me. I felt the blood run down both sides of my face. I had to act quickly or else this fight would be over before it had begun. I bucked and twisted in order to throw him off, but to no avail. I could think of only one tactic.

I shot my arms into the air, grabbed hold of him by his long hair, and pulled his head down to my face. I bit him hard on the earlobe. He let out a piercing scream and leapt off me. He covered his ear with both hands, through which blood flowed. He stood there, his face a mask of pain, and seemed to waiver. There was something in my mouth. I spat it out. It was a piece of his ear.

I was horrified. Had I just done *that*? I'm not surprised he was wavering. He was probably in shock and on the point of passing out. I thought I had gone too far.

I looked at Sophia, our lovely referee, to see if she would stop the fight, but she just looked on, eyes wide and obviously fascinated. She gave me a brief smile and a jerk of the head towards McNealy, as if to say: Go on, finish him.

She was right. I had to finish him. I couldn't waste another moment.

I lunged towards him from the ground and pushed him against the chest. We tumbled over together. I jumped onto his chest and pinned him beneath me. If I struck quickly, I could finish him off. However, my hesitation allowed him just enough time to recover. Also, his missing earlobe had caused him to erupt into fury. His face was twisted by hate and anger.

His fist shot out at me, taking me by surprise, and landed straight in my eye. I was knocked back. I fell off him and, momentarily stunned, collapsed to the ground. McNealy bounced up and gave me a hard and direct kick at my bollocks. I crumpled over in pain, holding my balls. He went to give me a good kicking again, but I rolled clear of his foot, grabbed hold of his leg, shot up, and gave a hard tug. He fell to the ground, with me still holding onto his leg.

He lay there, thrashing helpless around like a fish caught on a line. Blood was pouring out from where his ear lobe had been.

It was my turn to kick him in the balls. Once, twice, three times. He cried out loudly each time. His screwed up face betrayed the pain he was in. I thought he might submit, but it looked as if he might pass out first, and do that rather than surrender to me. I went to kick him one more time when the whistle blew. I let go of the leg and looked at the referee.

"This is a good fight," said Sophie with obvious relish. "Okay, you guys, to your corners and get your cudgels. Come straight back out and continue fighting."

I dashed over to my corner to get my cudgel. I thought if I got there fast enough, I would be able to get my cudgel and get back to him before he could get up. I got to my corner, grabbed the cudgel, and ran over to McNealy. He was still lying prostrate on the ground and in dire agony. Tears ran from his eyes.

A lightly accented voice erupted from the crowd, "Come on Freddie! Let him have it!" I glimpsed Keiko from the corner of my eye. Yes, I was going to let him have it. This beating would be for her pleasure. Something to make her moist.

I strode right up to McNealy and stood over him. I was facing the crowd. They were pressed up against the fence, eager to see me do it. There were shouts of encouragement. I saw a group of girls, their eyes wide with delight.

"Go on," screamed a pretty blonde haired beauty, "Finish him off. Don't be such a pussy." The other girls laughed. With such an audience, I was compelled to oblige.

I took hold of the cudgel with both hands, and with legs astride, lifted the cudgel high into the air. There was a gasp of breath from the crowd. I looked up at the group of girls. Their mouths were open expectantly. This was it. This is what they were waiting for. They wanted me to beat him savagely for their delight.

I swung down the cudgel, hitting him hard in the stomach. I heard the air being exhaled out of his mouth. His face screwed up in dire agony. Behind me, I heard a sharp intake of breath from Sophie. There was a round of applause. I heard shouts of encouragement. They were enjoying this. I saw Keiko looking on, smiling, her eyes wide and her mouth slightly open.

Suddenly I was falling to the ground.

There was a gasp from the crowd. With his last resource of strength that was positively superhuman, McNealy had kicked the feet from under me. I should have finished him off more swiftly. Again, I had hesitated. I lay on the ground, surprised more than stunned.

He jumped up off the ground, put his foot hard on my chest, pinning me down, and then leant over and adroitly undid my belt and trousers and pulled down my zip.

What the fuck!

I bucked and twisted in an effort to get free. He stepped back, grabbed hold of my ankles, hoisted my legs into the air, and then swiftly pulled off my trousers, which came off with embarrassing ease. There was a titter from the crowd. He grabbed hold of my ankles again, leant down, grabbed hold of the elastic band of my underpants, and gave it a hard tug. They slid along my legs and over my feet. He let go of my ankles. He picked up my trousers and underpants and threw them over the ring fence.

I was naked. There was general laughter at this turn of events.

One female shouted out, "Make them fight naked!" This was greeted with applause by other female members of the audience. McNealy's tactic was an attempt to undermine my confidence by humiliating me. However, it had the opposite effect.

The opportunity to fight naked in front of blood-thirsty girls was a recurring fantasy, one that I had masturbated to many times. For me, fighting naked did not undermine my confidence; it was a spur to fight. Out of the corner of my eye, I saw a group of women gazing wistfully at my genitalia and commenting. Let them. I was enjoying the attention. Now all I had to do was to give them a show that they will never forget.

I focussed on the fight. I saw McNealy run for the cudgel lying on the ground that I had been using. I shot up and ran to *his* corner, picked up the cudgel, turned, and then marched towards him. He waited for me in the centre of the court. This was it. This was to be a cudgel fight from now on.

As I came up to him, he swung his cudgel around in the air as if trying to get the feel of it. I did the same. We must have looked like a couple of prehistoric cave men getting ready to fight, especially as I was naked and we were both smeared with blood.

Suddenly, McNealy lunged forward and swung at my head. I ducked. I felt the rush of air as the cudgel narrowly missed. I stepped back. Again he came forward and again swung. I ran back until there was a reasonable distance between us. I then turned and faced him, cudgel gripped in both hands and ready for action.

Running towards me, he lifted his cudgel above his head and swung. I collapsed onto one knee and felt the whoosh of his cudgel above my head. I brought my cudgel as far back as it would go, and then, with all the force I could muster, swung it against his knee. There was a sickening thud, a cracking sound, and then a shriek from above me. He collapsed to the ground. I got up, raised the cudgel above my head, and glared down at him.

"For a grand," I said, with grim determination, "I am only too fucking willing to let you have it."

He looked up at me, his eyes full of malevolence and fear in equal measure. He said nothing. I really thought he would rather be beaten to death than submit to me.

Then, after a timeless moment, he mumbled, "I submit. I submit."

Sophie stepped forward with a smile on her face.

"Sorry," she said. "I couldn't hear a word of that. Please carry on with the fight."

"I submit! I submit!" he shouted.

The audience burst into applause.

Sophie came over, took hold of my hand, smiled at me, lifted my arm into the air, and shouted, "The winner!" There was another burst of applause.

Chapter 23

After the Fight

As the applause from the crowd died down, Sophie made an announcement, "There will now be a thirty minute break." Then turning to me, she said, "I hope you are hanging around. There might be a little *something* for you and the other winners later on."

"Like what?" I asked, intrigued.

"Watching you guys beat the shit out of one another is a complete turn on," she said, and then added a little coquettishly, "and everyone here has seen how well endowed you are." She glanced down at my penis. "There is someone here who wants to show her, um, how shall I put it, appreciation."

I smiled. "That'll be nice. I had no intention of going anywhere."

She laughed.

"Good. You won't be sorry." She then turned to the audience and declared there would be a thirty minute interval.

I left the court to applause. The butler appeared and handed me my trousers and underpants. I think I was supposed to put them back on. Instead, I folded them over my arm. I was enjoying the attention I was getting from the ladies in the audience, more than a few of whom were just staring at my genitalia.

Keiko ran up and threw her arms around me.

"Darling, you were wonderful," she exclaimed, kissing me hard on the lips. "Simply wonderful. And naked, too. Even better."

I returned the kiss and said, "I'm glad you enjoyed it. How is Sir Damon treating you?" I asked.

"Very well," she said. "He is the most charming host. When you're dressed, are you coming back down? I'm going to hang around and watch the other fights. This whole fighting with sticks is new to me. I wonder if they will introduce it in the Hope and Anchor."

"I hope not," I said firmly. "I could have killed him out there." Talking of McNealy made me think of him. I turned round to look at him lying on the ground. A doctor with a bag was knelt down by his side examining him.

"They have set up one of the rooms in the house as a first aid room," said Keiko. "The first fight ended up with one of the guys getting badly hit around the head with a stick. They had to carry him off in a stretcher."

"Fuck!" I said. "I hope he's all right."

"Me, too," said Keiko.

"You carry on watching the fights. I've been told I might have to hang around for a bit. I don't know why, but it is better to do as I'm told. I am being paid, after all."

"And you won, which means you will get paid an extra thousand pounds."

"Exactly." I kissed her on the lips and then made my way back to the mansion, with the butler leading the way. I felt a strange pleasure showing off my nakedness.

I asked the butler how badly hurt the fighter from the first fight was.

"Fuck knows," was all he said.

We entered the house. As we walked down a hallway towards the stairs, Sophie suddenly appeared out of a doorway.

"It's all right, Pearson," she said. "I'll take him back. You have a short rest." Pearson looked a little surprised, but obeyed his orders.

"Thank you, madam," he said, and then disappeared, leaving me alone with Sophia.

She looked me up and down and then smiled.

"Fucking hell," she said. "That was some fight. I have never seen a naked man fight before."

"Did you enjoy it?"

"Are you joking? It was fucking awesome." She stepped towards me and ran a finger down my cock. A touch of the Melanie about that. "I especially enjoyed this lovely thing waving about during the fight, and I don't think I was the only one, either." My cock stiffened slightly under her touch. She noticed it and smiled again. "Enjoy that?" she asked.

"Did you?" I replied. "Are you going to take me back to the room now?"

"Don't be so impatient. All in good time. Follow me."

She took me a short way along the corridor and then through a door. She closed the door and locked it behind her. I gazed around in some wonderment. Books covered nearly every space on the walls. I had never seen so many books outside of a public library. A huge painting of a Victorian gentleman looked down at us authoritatively from above the fireplace.

Sophie turned round and faced me.

"Christ, you look gorgeous. Naked, muscular, and covered in blood and bruises. What more can a woman want." She slipped out of her leather dress and panties. She looked gorgeous naked. Skinny with small breasts, long nipples, and long legs.

She walked up to me, touched my cock again, which swelled up appreciatively. She put her arms around me and kissed me passionately on the lips. I slid my arms around her waist and returned the kiss with equal fervour. She then went down on her knees, grabbed hold of my cock, and placed it into her mouth. Teasing my swollen cock with her tongue, it responded by twitching excitedly. I thought I was about to come when she pulled away.

She rose up, sat on the mahogany table in the middle of the room, spread her legs wide, and said, breathlessly, "Take me now."

I strode over, my penis thrust out before me like a battering ram. I grabbed hold of her waist, and pulled her wet cunt towards my prick. It slid in effortlessly. She threw her arms around my shoulders and hoisted herself onto me. I placed my hands under her buttocks and held her up. I started pumping as her hips started gyrating.

"God! You were fucking great out there," she panted. "All that blood and nakedness. I thought I was going to have an orgasm on the court." I kept pumping. I was enjoying this. This is why I fought. "I wanted you to hit him over and over again."

Then her back arched and she cried out, "Oh fuck, yes!" and then she came. I ejaculated. One hard thrust and my spunk came flying out. Her body convulsed several times and then relaxed. I relaxed, too. Her breathing was ragged. She let go of me and I let go of her. I stepped back from her, my cock sliding out of her pussy.

"Shit! I'm covered in blood." She went to a side table, took off the table cloth, and wiped herself clean with it. She then dressed. "Come with me," she said, "I'll take you back to your room."

On entering the room, the others gazed at my nakedness in some surprise. There were a handful of comments and several wolf whistles, which I ignored. I went into the bedroom, undressed, and then took a shower. As the water flowed over me, I watched as my blood trickled down the plug hole. It reminded me of the shower scene in Hitchcock's *Psycho*.

I stepped out of the shower unit, towelled myself down, and then got dressed. I had a fresh pair of underpants and trousers in my bag. Once dressed, I gazed at myself in the mirror. No doubt about it, I had been in the wars: A bruised cheek, the beginnings of a black eye, and a cut lip.

Looking at my state made me think of McNealy. I thought of his earlobe and the feel of it in my mouth. It was rubbery. The memory of it made me nauseous. Bile began to force its way up from my stomach. I rushed to the sink and vomited. Feeling wretched, I propped myself up against the sink. A second lot of bile forced its way up. I vomited again. I switched on the tap and let the water wash away the vomit. What in God's good name could have compelled me to bite off a man's earlobe? The nausea passed, but an acrid taste of digestive acid remained in my throat. More than anything, I wanted a drink of water.

I ambled back into the main room with my bag and flopped down into an armchair. No-one spoke. I sat back and relaxed. The comfort of the chair, the sun streaming through the window, the languid silence of the room, and the exhaustion of the fight, caused me to doze and then to drift into a deep sleep. I dreamt.

I dreamt of Melanie. I was in the Hope and Anchor. I had beaten McNealy to the ground and he had slapped the floor in submission. The referee stepped forward, but it wasn't Mitch, it was Melanie. She was wearing a short backless dress with a plummeting cleavage. One breast had slipped out and I noticed her nipple was fully erect.

She came up to me with a cudgel and said, with a wicked gleam in her eye, "Use this to finish him off." She handed it to me and then withdrew into the shadows, laughing nervously, waiting for me to cause

McNealy real hurt.

I looked down at McNealy. He was lying on the ground with fear in his eyes. He started pleading for mercy, for me not to kill him. I got my cock out and started masturbating. I came. McNealy had morphed into his father. A huge blob of cum spurted over his face, covering him like a mask, so that he couldn't breath. He went blue and started gasping for air. I lifted up the cudgel to finish him off.

"Yes! Yes! Yes! Kill him! Mash up his face!" Melanie screamed with unrestrained sexual excitement.

I awoke with a start. The shadows had shifted. I supposed I had been asleep for some time. Far from being refreshed, my eyes were heavy and my mind dull. I crossed my legs to hide the fact that I had an erection. I thought about how Melanie would have loved today. I looked around the room. The grandfather clock in the corner said five thirty. I must have been asleep for an hour and a half.

I looked at the fighters arrayed about the room. They were all fully dressed now, but battered and bruised and exhausted. A few fighters were missing. Had they been taken to the first aid room? Had there been fatalities? Those cudgels are a brutal and stupid idea. I hoped I would never see those again, let alone use one. I thought again about McNealy and his earlobe. The thought would not go away.

What had I done?

Sir Damon Nicholls came in carrying a briefcase.

"Gentleman," he said. "I would like to thank you for participating in today's fights. You all performed extremely well. For those of you who lost, you are free to go downstairs, join the main party, and help yourself to food and drink. In short: Enjoy yourselves. The rest of you, those who won, would you please stay behind for a short while."

Those who lost rose up and walked out the room. The room seemed a lot larger now that it was only half full. The remaining eight of us waited expectantly. Sir Damon spoke again.

"Congratulations on your victories." Sir Damon put the briefcase on the table and opened it. "Gather round and collect your prize money? Once you have done so, hang around a little longer, I will want to say just one more thing."

We all gathered round the table. The briefcase was full of bundled up money, each bundle worth one thousand pounds. He dished it out like Santa Claus dolling out presents at a Christmas party. I took my bundle, checked it, and then placed it in my bag. Eventually we had all been given our money.

Sir Damon said, "Now if you want, you can go downstairs. The party is in full swing. Help yourself to drinks and food. On the other hand, on the premises, there is a very attractive young lady who enjoyed your performances tonight, and is only too keen to, how shall I put it, show her *appreciation*." He turned to the door and called out. "My dear, you may come in now."

The door opened and a girl entered. I stared in disbelief.

Melanie!

She wore a short white dress that clung to her body like a second skin. It was obvious she wasn't wearing a bra. Her nipples protruded effortlessly through the flimsy fabric. Every pair of eyes in the room swivelled in her direction.

"Hi guys," she said, with a broad smile on her face. Everyone mumbled a reply. She then looked directly at me. "Freddie. How are you?"

"Fine. You?"

"Fine, also."

"Glad to see you two know one another," said Sir Damon, looking a little surprised. "Now, if you like, you may all accompany Melanie to a private room where she will *entertain* you. If not, follow me and we can join the party."

Sir Damon left the room leaving all eight of us alone with Melanie. We looked sheepishly around the room, not sure what to do next. One left to join the party, leaving seven of us.

"Okay, you guys want to follow me?" said Melanie, taking control.

Like dwarves behind a not-so Snow White, we followed her out of the room, down a wood panelled hallway, up the grand staircase to the next floor, and then along another wood panelled hallway. She finally stopped at a door, opened it, and ushered us through.

We found ourselves in a large bedroom. In a corner, an old fashioned wash basin was fixed to the wall. Beside it was a small set of drawers on which lay a neatly folded towel. Through a high sash window, the late afternoon sun poured in onto the one item that dominated the room: An immense four poster oak bed.

It was ornately carved with twisted posts. At the end, embossed on a giant headboard, was a coat of arms. The drapes, which were of heavy green velvet, were tied back. The mattress was thick, heavy and massive. It looked as if it could have accommodated all nine of us and still have space for more.

Melanie closed the door behind her, turned around and leaned against it, as if ensuring we wouldn't change our minds and leave. She needn't have bothered. The air was heavy with expectation. Only an idiot would have wanted to leave.

As it turned out, all expectations were fully met.

Chapter 24

The Final Touch

"Don't mind if I undress, do you?" she said without expecting or even waiting for an answer. Melanie kicked off her high heeled shoes and unzipped the back of her dress. Because it clung so tightly to her body, she slowly and carefully eased herself out of the dress until she emerged like a butterfly from its chrysalis. Once she slipped off her panties, she stood before us, naked.

How many times had I seen her get undressed? *Countless times.* Yet as I watched her undress before six gawping strangers, I felt as if I were watching a girlfriend perform in a strip club. Her manner of undressing was deliberately provocative. She undressed with her audience in mind.

Yet, she was offering more than mere titillation.

Getting naked was just the start.

With an almost feline elegance, she sauntered over to the bed, the men in front of her parting like the Red Sea.

"I would just like to say something," she said, sitting down on the end of the bed and making eye contact with each man in the room. "I watched you guys fight. You were awesome. You really were. You made a lot of women out there so fucking horny, including me. So come on. Fuck me. One at a time. Two at a time. Gang bang me. I don't care. I am at your disposal. Think of me as a whore and do what you like with me." The room sank into silence as men, who had fearlessly faced other men in physical combat only hours before, became like shy schoolboys when confronted by a naked and confident woman.

"It might be an idea if you all took off your clothes," said Melanie, encouragingly.

Everyone in the room, except for me, hurriedly removed their clothes. Once they were naked, she waved them over and they advanced towards her.

I didn't. I remained where I was and fully dressed. I don't know why. Maybe sex with Sophie had satiated me? There is only so much one man can deliver, after all. Maybe it was because Melanie had once been my girlfriend and I didn't like sharing her with others? Maybe at heart I am a voyeur and I prefer to watch? Unsure of the reason, I remained aloof from the events that unfolded before my eyes.

The men crowded around her. One man was grabbed by Melanie and pulled towards her. She placed his cock in her mouth and started sucking it.

"Jesus Christ! That's fucking lovely," he said, gripping her shoulders tightly. I recognised him as the sinewy guy with a foul mouth and covered with tattoos who had earlier commented on Sir Damon's wealth, "Keep going girl. Don't fucking stop."

She didn't. As her head bobbed, his cock rapidly became engorged with blood until it was fully erect, at which point she removed her lips and gazed at it admiringly. Whether she was admiring its firmness, or the girl's name tattooed on it, I couldn't tell.

She then pulled another man towards her and did the same. As she sucked on his cock, the men moved in closer, pressing against her. She serviced one cock after another until they were all fully erect.

She selected what appeared to be the largest cock, whose owner was a swarthy young muscular man with flowing black hair, grabbed hold of his waist and drew him right up close to her, and placed his cock in her mouth. She started licking and sucking it. He screwed up his eyes as if a wave of ecstasy was sweeping over him. Suddenly, she withdrew her head, and as she did so, he came, copiously, all over her face. She closed her eyes as his cum hit her full on. It lay on her like a white creamy face mask. The mask began to run as it slid down her face, dripping off her nose and chin.

There was a silence in the room. Through a mask of semen, she looked up with large doe-eyes, her face an expression of pure bliss.

Melanie rose up and dashed over to the sink. She washed her face, dried it with the towel, and then sat back down on the end of the bed.

"A bit salty," she said, to everyone's amusement, "but nice otherwise. C'mon guys. Let's get back to business." All six of the remaining naked men gathered back around, their erect cocks pointed directly upwards, as if proudly proclaiming their owners' virility. She stroked several, kissed one, and placed another into her mouth, sliding her lips along the erect shaft, teasing it with her tongue. As she did so, the others ran their hands through her hair, over her body, stroking her skin, fondling her breasts and teasing her nipples. She was embedded in a slowly gyrating mass of male human flesh. It was a scene of utter dissoluteness, an orgy of Ancient Roman proportions, and in the centre was Melanie, relishing every debauched minute.

The sinewy tattooed man gave an anguished whimper and then ejaculated, squirting cum over Melanie's left shoulder and down her back. Melanie carried on as if nothing had happened. The man's cock she was sucking erupted in her mouth. She carried on sucking as cum dribbled out of the sides of her mouth like fresh cream. When she was finished, she removed the cock from her mouth and wiped her lips with her hand.

Melanie stood up and climbed onto the bed on all fours, doggy style.

"Does one of you want to take me from behind?" she asked, spreading her legs and shoving her arse into the air as if in invitation.

A young man with blonde hair and blue eyes got on the bed behind her and started rubbing his cock on the crack of her arse. As he did so, she pulled a tall black man with a shaved head forward and slid his hard cock into her mouth. She started to noisily suck it. The blond youth behind her inserted his cock into Melanie's pussy. It slid in and then he started thrusting. With each thrust, Melanie's body jolted, and the black man whose cock was being sucked, also jolted. Bizarrely, it conjured up in my mind the image of a single machine: All parts working in unison and building up to a climax. The ultimate sex machine. I half expected a steam valve to be let off once they reached ejaculation.

As all three were lost in their debauched labours, an Asian man, with a Samurai decapitating a prisoner tattooed on his back, was standing beside the bed, eagerly viewing the spectacle in front of him and furiously wanking. Suddenly, he came and cum spurted out and splattered the right side of Melanie's face and hair.

While the cum dripped off Melanie and on to the bed sheets, the black man in front climaxed first. With a sharp intake of breath, he came, his body jolting violently. His eyes closed as he became lost in his own orgasm. Simultaneously, the blond youth behind, both hands clutching Melanie's waist, gave two aggressive thrusts and then, with his body convulsing, also came.

Melanie continued to greedily suck on the black cock in her mouth, her cheeks sharply drawn inwards with each suck, extracting the last tiny drop of cum, which she then swallowed. She withdrew the cock from her mouth and wiped her mouth with the back of her hand. The youth behind withdrew the cock from Melanie's pussy and collapsed back onto the bed, a look of utter satisfaction plastered across his exhausted face. She looked at the last of the men who had not ejaculated.

He was a stocky man with a slight paunch and two cauliflower ears. He stood to one side and was aggressively masturbating. His cock was huge and hard in his hand. It suddenly erupted and spurted cum all over Melanie's body.

"Fantastic," she laughed out loud, smearing the cum all over her stomach and rubbing it into her breasts. "The final touch."

She was now kneeling on the bed. Her beautiful body with its flawless skin covered in cum which glistened in the dying sunlight. It slowly ran over her breasts, her stomach, her back, her face, and even clung to her hair.

I had found watching Melanie having sex with a group of male fighters sensational and arousing. She had fully satisfied her sexual desire and had provided me with the most erotic spectacle imaginable.

I thought Sophie, for all sexual purposes, had drained me completely. But no. Straining to escape the confines of my trousers was the largest erection I swear I have ever experienced. I thought it might burst the stitching. I was breathing heavily and on the verge of ejaculation.

Melanie stood up, went to a side table and drank a glass of water. She ran the water in the sink and then after soaking a flannel and lathering it with soap, washed the cum off her body and out of her hair as best as she could. She then towelled her self dry. The men, having been fully satisfied, silently got dressed.

Melanie, still naked, came over to me, put her arms around my neck and kissed me on the lips. Oh! That tiny mouth. Those soft lips. The memories came flooding back. She darted her small tongue into my mouth. I parried, and then I was inside her mouth, licking the back of her teeth. As I did so, I wondered if I could taste the remnants of the other men, the salty cum she had so freely allowed to be ejaculated into her mouth by the men now standing around us.

"Freddie? Don't you want to fuck me?"

"I do want to fuck you."

"Well, get your clothes off and come and fuck me."

I got undressed and left my clothes in an untidy heap on the floor. I slid my arms around her waist and pulled her to me. I again kissed her on the lips.

I ran my hands down her back and then over the round hills of her buttocks. I relished the softness of her skin and the warmth of her flesh. I felt my hard cock push against her pussy.

"Shall we...." she said, indicating the bed.

I slipped a finger inside her wet cunt. She gasped. I began to stroke her clitoris with my thumb, the way she always used to like it. She shuddered.

"I loved your fight, today," she said, her eyes closed. She opened them and looked directly at me. "Why did you wash the blood off? It quite suited you. It made you look quite the savage."

"Next time, I'll keep it smeared all over myself."

"Please do. It was lovely." She then lay down on the bed, spread her legs apart, leaving her cunt gaping. My cock was fully erect and quivering. "Come on," she said. "I can see you're ready."

I lay down on top of her and slid my cock effortlessly into her wet cunt. She threw her arms around me, pulling me close to her, and I started pumping: Slowly at first, and then increasing the pace until I was going at her energetically. I could hear the juices in her body squelching every time I thrust inside her. Her ragged breathing was loud.

Melanie and I held each other's naked bodies tightly, her smooth skin and warm flesh pressed hard against mine. I ran my hands over her soft buttocks. I closed my eyes, relishing Melanie's body and thinking of her having sex with every fighter she could find: Today, tomorrow, and in the past.

My cock continued to swell and harden. I plunged it into her wet cunt, each thrust making her groan with undisguised ecstasy. I came. Her cunt muscles gripped my swollen cock tightly. I exploded inside her. A huge gush.

She arched her back, let out a piercing shriek, her body shuddered, and then collapsed back onto the bed, exhausted and satisfied.

I let out a long drawn-out breath and then I slumped on top of Melanie. We were both panting. I wanted to lie there, like we used to, but I was aware we had an audience, and anyway, I was no longer her lover, but a fighter to be fucked, like any other.

I rose up and stood by the bed. Melanie just lay there looking contented. She looked up at everyone, ran a hand over her belly, and smiled. Her legs were immodestly wide apart. She unashamedly displayed her cunt.

"Thanks you, guys," she said. "Today was fun. Now I must go and clean myself up."

To my great surprise, everyone applauded. I did, too. She had, after all, given quite a performance.

For both Melanie and me, it had been quite a day. Exhausting, but exhilarating. We had both worked hard.

I would have liked to have hung around for the party, but it was already evening and Keiko wanted to go home. We said goodbye to Sir Damon, thanked him for a wonderful day, and left. We offered Melanie a lift home.

By the time we reached the outskirts of London, it was dusk. There was little traffic. Keiko pulled into the fast lane and pressed down on the accelerator.

"So did you enjoy my fight?" I asked.

"You were wonderful," replied Keiko.

"Did you get laid, afterwards?"

"Did you?"

"I asked first."

"Yes."

"Who was it? Someone I know?"

"You should. You beat the crap out of him earlier on today."

"McNealy!" I blurted out, starring at her in amazement. "Tell me you are pulling my leg."

Keiko laughed. "Not at all. After you gave him a thrashing, they took him to the first aid room. I was curious, so I followed. Everyone thought you had torn off his earlobe, but it was only a tiny part of it and not as much as you probably thought. The doctor stitched it up there and then. However, Sir Damon said he would pay for plastic surgery to get it looking as good as new. They took him to a sitting room and left him alone to recover. I took the opportunity to slip in and introduce myself.

"Watching you both fight had made me horny, so I took out his cock, gave him a blow job, and just before he came, I straddled him and we had sex. I felt after you had bitten his earlobe off, it was the least I could do."

"Not fuck him is the least you could have done."

"Okay. I'm sorry," she said, with out any pretence of sincerity. "Now about you. Did you get laid?"

"Yes."

"Was she good?"

"Very much so."

"So the fight was worth it, then?"

"Yes."

"And what about Freddie: Was he any good?"

Melanie leant forward from the back seat so that she was between us.

"Of all the ones I fucked today, Freddie was easily the best. He fought beautifully as well, so I was well and truly wet and slippery. Nothing like watching loads of guys fighting to get the slip and slide going."

"Where were you?" I said to Melanie. "I didn't see you in the crowd."

"I was watching from the first floor."

"Why from there? Why not come down and watch at the front?"

"Why do you think?" said Keiko.

"Don't tell me you were being fucked from behind by someone?" I said to Melanie.

"You got it in one. I was being fucked from behind by a fighter called Tom Goldfield."

"I don't know him."

"He's a good fuck. A good fighter, as well. I had an orgasm just as I thought you were going to beat your opponent with that stick. And you naked, too. I think all fighters should go naked."

"So we all had a good day, then."

There was a universal agreement it had been a good day. I was happy McNealy's ear was not as badly damaged as I thought it would be, but the memory of it still made me queasy. Perhaps I should leave the fight game. Addictions can be beaten. Maybe I can live my fantasy through Keiko. I'd sleep on it, but before I slept tonight, I would need to satisfy Keiko.

It had been a good day. I had Keiko beside me, Melanie in the back, and Sophia's telephone number in my pocket. My next fight is in three weeks time. I might just give Sophie a call and invite her along. She would love the Fucking Room.

Keiko pulled off the London Orbital motorway and headed towards Docklands and home.

About the Author

B.B. Anderson was born in 1958, in Bromley, a borough of London, which is where H.G. Wells was born: a fact that both inspires and weighs heavily on him. He has had nine short stories published, six of which were published in the late and much lamented sex magazine, *Forum*. *Fighting Hard* is his first novel. He has just completed another, which, alas, is not erotic, but he is soon to start a third novel, which *is* erotic. Along with modern erotic fiction, B.B. Anderson draws his inspiration from writers of the past, such as Anais Nin, Henry Miller, D.H. Lawrence, and the Marquis de Sade.

About the Publisher

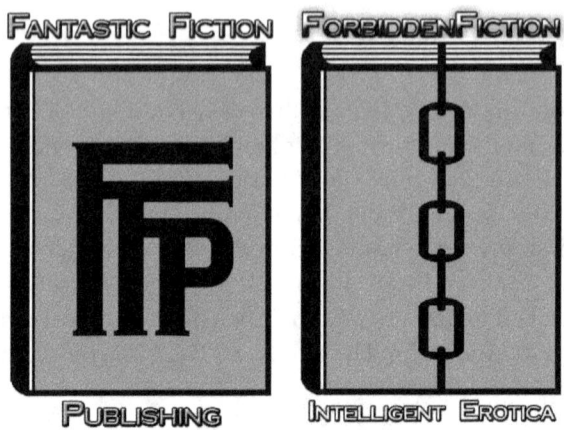

ForbiddenFiction.com is a publisher devoted to writing that breaks the boundaries of original erotic fiction. Our stories combine intense sexuality with quality writing. Stories at ForbiddenFiction.com not only arouse readers through sensations, but also engage them emotionally and mentally through storytelling as well-crafted as the sex is hot.

ForbiddenFiction.com is also designed to be a social reading environment. You'll have fun even if just reading the latest post each day, yet you will have the chance for so much more. Readers and authors can be part of ongoing discussions of specific works and individual authors as well as more general topics.

Sign up for a FREE Membership today at ForbiddenFiction.com

www.ingramcontent.com/pod-product-compliance
Lightning Source LLC
Chambersburg PA
CBHW071911220626
47052CB00002B/308